in case of emergency press

We are proud to acknowledge the Traditional Owners of country
throughout Australia and to recognise their continuing
connection to land, waters, and culture.
We pay our respects to their Elders.

We support recognition, reconciliation, and reparation.

NOT MISSING A
SINGLE THING

IAN JAMIESON

in case of emergency press
https://icoe.com.au
Travancore, Victoria
Australia

Published by in case of emergency press 2024

ISBN: 978-0-6458496-7-7

ACKNOWLEDGEMENTS

Not easy to get a first novel published in Australia. And that would not have happened without the people from **in case of emergency press**. So, a big thank you to everyone there.

DEDICATION

I'd like to thank my wife Lisa and my son Gareth. Their quiet support and encouragement have always been with me; without it, I doubt I'd have a novel with my name on it. I also need to give a special thank you to Alan, my Pomeranian friend, who has been beside me for the writing of every single word, only ever needing a pat, cuddle or a treat in return.

Thanks team.

TABLE OF CONTENTS

ρ

NOT MISSING A SINGLE THING

IAN JAMIESON

A MANDARIN AND IDIOT SIR

This isn't part of the story, at least not the part that I really want to tell you about. But you're going to get it anyway! That last sentence is the new me, sounding all strong and certain. I'm not always comfortable with the new me, still getting used to it. I have to tell you this bit because it's the horrible thing that led to something better. It's like the story my mum told me about one of her friends who was in a car crash and broke both of her legs. Obviously that's the bad bit. But in the hospital she fell in love with her doctor and they planned to get married when she got better and live happily ever after. That's the good bit. So, the bit I'm about to tell you is like my car crash story.

I've also got to tell you this car crash stuff because there's this nasty dark lump sitting in my brain, bubbling and festering away, and I just have to get rid of it, get it out of my system. It's like the time when I was nine or ten and I ate way too much chocolate cake, chana daal and ice cream at *his* birthday party and didn't feel better until I was sick in the smelly outdoor toilet.

I should mention here that this isn't easy for me to do, not easy at all, even if it is my 'car crash' that led to something better. Bit embarrassing and painful it is. I could really use some assistance, a bit of a helping hand just to get things started would be great. So, Lord Krishna if you could give me some help I'd really appreciate it. If you do that Krishna, I'll put all my sweets for a whole week in front of the picture mum has of you. Miss Windsor, who used to be my sixth class teacher, encouraged me to get this done, telling me it would make all the other hard bits easier. And Miss Windsor is someone worth listening to.

Later, after hours of agony and buckets of brain-sweat, mum said instead of asking Krishna for help, it should have been Saraswati because she's the Hindu goddess in charge of language, music, art and... and other creative sort of stuff. No wonder

1

Krishna ignored me! Maybe he also thought the offer of sweets was a bribe and not the reward I wanted it to be, and being a god he probably wouldn't respond well to bribery. I do, however. I'd never heard of Saraswati but wrote her name down for later on. Then I promised her Krishna's sweets.

Okay, deep breath. Here's my car crash story, my vomiting in the smelly toilet... deep breath, deep breath, deep breath...

It smacked me on the back of the head. It didn't hurt, but it made my running stall as if I was some super-fast car that just ran out of petrol. They'd blocked off the laneway; three in front of me, just waiting, cutting off escape while the other three who'd been chasing me caught up. A mandarin, it was a mandarin that had hit the back of my head. It stuck there for a moment before its squelchy splat onto the ground.

I'm a fast runner, which comes in very handy I can tell you, but there were always times when it wasn't fast enough. This was the third time I'd been chased and caught. At least in that school it was. I'd escaped dozens and dozens of times, which sounds like good odds in my favour, but it all means nothing when they catch you. Six of them there were, and I didn't know the name of a single one. And they didn't know my name, though that didn't stop them calling me names. It didn't matter how often teachers told me 'sticks and stones will break your bones, but words will never hurt you', because I can tell you that it's absolute rubbish, because words hurt, the sort of hurt that keeps on hurting.

The day the mandarin went splat on the back of my head was a Friday, it was always a Friday after school, like it was some ritual start to their weekend, a fun beginning to two days off. I think I was the only kid who didn't look forward to the ringing of the Friday afternoon bell. I'd get all sweaty-nervous watching the jerky minute hand on the wall clock behind Sir's desk. The closer it got to three o'clock the more I was certain I could hear its ticking picking up pace, pulsing like a panicked heartbeat, the minutes, then seconds rushing to get me. This particular Friday I was concentrating so hard on the clock, feeling more and more sweaty-nervous, that I seemed to disappear into the ugly world of what was coming my way. And in that moment someone was out of my desk and they were rushing for the door, rushing to escape. My desk was at the back of the room and this was a good thing because people had to turn around to throw stuff at me, but a bad thing if someone was trying to escape. That's why Sir caught them by the collar just as they got to the door, just as they almost made it. When Sir dragged them back to the front of the class, I felt my collar tight against my throat as Sir yelled, "Stand still you worm!" and then it was me he was yelling at, me the class was laughing at.

Sir leant across his desk and got his cane. "Should give you six of the best," he said, "running like a loony, knocking a desk over. Can't have it. Should be six of the best, but you can only have three. But I'll make them count." And he caned me three times on my right hand and it hurt and I didn't want to cry, really tried not to, but it did hurt and I did cry. And crying didn't make things any better.

A week before Sir caned me, I had been to see him in his office. I had never been to see Sir before, had never wanted to, but was following my mum's advice. I had a long note from her to give to Sir. I knocked on the door to his office and the door flew open like there was some rush for him to see who was there. It was a small room, tiny even, barely large enough for a desk and an old armchair. A square birdcage sat on the desk, two budgies motionless and silent on their perch. The one window was papered over in old newspaper. Cigarette smoke filled the room, different pictures of Surf Lifesavers pinned to the walls.

"What?" he barked. "What is it?" As soon the door swung open, I knew I'd made a mistake, it wasn't something I did, I didn't stand up and speak out, I didn't like to make a fuss; nothing good ever came of it, best stay quiet, best stay hidden. But I was following mum's advice, following it because she said she'd come to the school if I didn't. And I couldn't, just couldn't have that. "What is it?" Sir said again, "Cat got your tongue?"

I told Sir how I was being chased and bullied and terrified after school, though what I actually said was,"I'm having a few problems after school." I didn't tell him it was sometimes on the way to school, often in the playground and very often in his class; I didn't tell him these things because, unlike my mum, I didn't have very high hopes of any success. Any hope, really. With good reason. I'll give you an example.

It was a Monday, I know that for certain because each Monday would start with Sir telling the class about the dozens of drowning swimmers he and his lifesaver friends had pulled from the raging surf. I'd only been at the school a couple of weeks when two big boys grabbed my left arm and held it down on my desk. "Let's do it," one of them said and giggled. Sir was writing on the board but turned around when he heard the raised voices and scuffling, saw what was going on and said, "Now, now," before turning back to writing on the board. A tall and very pretty girl got some crayons out of her pencil case. "Hold the thing still," she said, and on the end of my arm drew a smudgy mouth, a single line for a nose and two wonky circles for eyes. "Look Sir," the girl squealed, "look Sir, we made a sock puppet and didn't even need a sock. Look Sir!" Sir turned around and looked at my left arm that the two boys were waving about, checked the clock behind his desk and told the class it was time for recess.

And that was one of my reasons for not having any hope. Sir was not the sort of teacher to help me; I could have knocked on his office door and stood in front of him dressed and looking like one of his Surf Lifesavers and all he would have done was look at my arms, laugh and tell me, "Don't reckon you'd ever be able to paddle a surfboard!" But I had no choice. So, there I was standing in the doorway to his office telling him I had a few problems.

"Hmm, a few problems, eh?" he said while rubbing his chin like he was giving it some deep consideration. I looked past Sir and could see that the budgies hadn't moved an inch. I felt sorry for myself, but more sorry for the two birds. Sir took a packet of cigarettes out of his shirt pocket, got one out and lit it. "Hmm," he said again as he drew deeply on the cigarette. I kept looking at the red glow on the end of the cigarette, gave it all my concentration so that it became the red dot, the bindi, that mum used to wear in the middle of her forehead before all the shouting and crying took it away. I was happy when mum wore the bindi. But Sir wouldn't leave me alone. "Oi, you listening to me? It's top advice I'm giving you here. I said, you need to toughen up a bit. See those Surf Lifesavers behind you?" He swept his arm across the pictures pinned to the back wall. Ash fell from his cigarette. "Bet those blokes had some problems growing up. But look at them now, bronzed heroes each and every one of them. You see, in Australia we Aussies are mighty tough, like the Anzacs. So, like I said, toughen up matey, try to be a bit more Aussie. So, that's my advice Ron, toughen up!" Sir dropped his cigarette, crushed it with his shoe and the bindi was long gone.

I told him I was born in Australia. He looked at me a moment, then said, "Hmm, maybe. Maybe. Doesn't matter anyway. Toughen up Ron." He then shut the door to his office. I didn't give him the note from my mum. And my name isn't Ron.

After Sir had caned me that Friday, after I'd cried in front of a sniggering class, I had hoped that things wouldn't get any worse. But then I was being chased, my running stalled by the splat of a mandarin, and all escape cut off as they closed in on me. I was in the cobbled laneway that ran behind rows of rundown houses. High brick walls lined each side of the laneway, rubbish scattered everywhere. The six boys closed in on me. Someone grabbed my right arm and twisted it behind my back and kicked my feet out from under me, so that I crashed onto the greasy and cold cobbles. Someone else pushed my face into the stones, my cheekbone grinding hard and hurting. I could smell oil and mould, things decayed and rotten, a sad laneway where a thousand bad things had happened.

"Today is your reward day, a yummy feast day," one of them said. Someone else picked up part of the mandarin and was rubbing it into my scrunched-up face. "Nice fresh fruit, eh? Fresh fruit to clear up your skin." They all laughed.

"Oh, hey. Brilliant," one of them called, sounding happy and excited. "Oh yeah, oh yeah! Over here, bring him here. Over here. Come on!" I was dragged to my feet and pulled to the other side of the laneway. "That's got to be from one of Ando's greyhounds. It's huge."

"And fresh. Fresh and warm. Your lucky day." Again I was thrown onto the cobbles of the laneway. This time someone had their boot on the side of my face, someone else still twisting my right arm, my left arm free but useless.

"Eat it up, eat up what Ando's left. It's especially for the likes of you. Eat it up!" And then all six were chanting, "Eat it up, eat it up."

"Tell us it's yummy, tell us it smells yummy and we'll let you go. Tell us it smells yummy!"

When I said nothing my face was pushed into the mound, the still warm mound, and I could feel it smeared all over my face and smell a smell that would stay with me for days and days.

"Now tell us it's yummy, or we'll serve you seconds. Tell us!" Whoever had been twisting my right arm let it go and I was able to sit up a little. "Ah, ah, don't wipe it off. It's a perfect colour." I looked away, trying not to see any of their faces, lest they see it a challenge to goad them on, because I already knew that cruelty likes to feed on cruelty.

"Yummy," I said. There was fading laughter as they walked away.

I should have kept my mouth shut. They'd finished with me, so I should have kept quiet. It's what I normally did, what I *always* did. But not this time. I was on my feet, yelling as loud as I could, calling them every swear word I could think of. Some of the swear words were the worst kind you could imagine, words I'd heard *him* use when he was working on his car. A screen door at the back of one of the houses opened and a lady with very long grey hair, dressed in a bright red dressing gown, stood on the back verandah. "Oi you, shut it up. Shut it up you little foul mouth," she said. But I did not shut it up. And I'm not sure I could have, even if I'd wanted to. I was yelling and swearing at six boys who'd chased me and rubbed dog poo in my face, I was swearing because Sir had caned me and because Sir was an idiot, I was yelling and swearing for always being picked on, always left out, I was swearing for the years of being frightened, for never having a friend, and I was screaming and swearing because *he* wasn't there anymore.

They came back to get me. Of course they did. What was I expecting? Just as they got to me the lady in the red dressing gown disappeared behind her screen door. "What did you call us?" one of them asked. I started repeating some of the best swear words when one of them grabbed me in a headlock. "Dak him," someone else said. "Get his pants off. Undies too, yeah undies too. Teach him good and proper we will. Off, off, off!"

I tried to stop them, squirmed and kicked as much as I could, but six against one isn't much of a contest. When they got my pants and underpants off, all my resistance, swearing and anger left me and I was hollow and empty, all my fight gone, defeated. "Told ya it'd all be the same colour, had to be all the same," one of them said. As they turned to leave, another waved my clothes at me and said, "You can pick these up at school on Monday."

I don't know how long I lay there, maybe minutes, maybe hours, and I don't remember a single thing that ran through my mind. It was like everything had been switched off and my head was just dark and blank. Then the lady in the red dressing gown was leaning over me, holding out an old and torn towel. "Here, take this and hop it home as quick as you can. And no more muckin' around with your mates."

I didn't go back to school again for almost two weeks. I'd hang around the local park, sometimes the library or shopping centre, it didn't really matter where because anywhere was better than school. Then the school called mum. I told mum the story of what happened in the laneway. I had to tell her the whole story because my mum is an expert interrogator whose eyes can see all the way into my head, finding the little part where I tell lies.

Down to the school we went, mum full steam ahead, me praying I could disappear and come back sometime later. It was after school, kids heading home, but mum found Sir in his smoky little office.

"Well, well my lovely, what is it I can do for you?" Sir said when he opened the door. I had a feeling that this was not going to go well. "Care to step into my office? Oh, you're there too Ron. Been off a couple of days, eh?"

Mum did not step into Sir's office. When mum told him about the laneway and being bullied, Sir waved his arm across the photos of the Surf Lifesavers and then gave the same speech he'd given me. When he finished, things were very quiet for a few moments. It was when Sir started grinning and looking mum up and down that she slapped him. It knocked a cigarette out of his mouth and, Krishna forgive me, it was most lovely to behold. This was definitely not how my mum usually behaved. I was shocked, but in a nice way because, as I said, it was lovely to behold. I had been wrong about my feeling; I think things had gone rather well.

A week later we were driving past the school and that too was lovely, because I was finished with that school and we were heading out of town. Mum had been planning for us to move, some small town up the coast, but slapping Sir had speeded things up. Yippee, hurray! It was such a pity, I thought, that most places no matter how small seemed to have a school; such a waste because I for one could've done without them.

"I guess it'll be another school for me, a new school?" I asked mum. I knew the answer, but it didn't hurt to try my luck.

"Of course," she answered, "and we'll keep changing places, changing schools, until we find a place where they stop doing it. Or where you can stop them doing it." I didn't much like hearing that last sentence of mum's, thought there was an awful burden in it, much too much for me to ever carry.

As we drove past the school, leaving Sir behind, I didn't feel the least bit sorry, happy to go I was. I had no regrets, nothing to be sad about. Except one thing. And it's something that still bothers me. Late one night I would like to have crept back into the school. In dark shadows I'd pause a moment and send a prayer to Kartikeya, the destroyer of evil and protector of all living things. I'd smash the window to Sir's tiny, smoky office, climb in and steal the square cage with the two budgies. On the way out, I would pull down and tear up the photos of the Surf Lifesavers. The budgies would chatter away and dance on their perch. But I didn't do any of that because the me that I am now didn't exist then. A pity because all those years after driving past that school I might now be the sort of person to do something like that. I'm still not capable of fighting off six bullies, but I wouldn't say, "Yummy." Maybe it wasn't an awful burden that would be too much for me to ever carry.

There you have it: my car crash story!

When I mentioned to mum how I'd used the story about her friend with the two broken legs who fell in love with her doctor and how they got married and lived happily ever after, she screwed up her face and was quiet for a few moments. "Hmm," she said. "It didn't end happily ever after. He was already married with five children." For the sake of what I've been telling you, I'd like you to stick with my car crash story leading to something good. Please ignore the married with five kids thing, don't let it ruin my example; only told you in the spirit of proving how totally honest I am, and in case you should ever meet my mum because she'd be likely to tell you if the topic came up.

Miss Windsor was right, not full right, but a bit right anyway. The telling did make me feel better, but it was like that time I ate too much chocolate cake, chana daal and ice cream. That time I had to vomit to feel better, but was still left with a bitter taste in my mouth.

It has taken me and my special pencil ages to write all this down. (Yes, I have a special pencil!) When I finished I took a moment to thank Saraswati. I also decided that mandarins should become one of my favourite fruits, because if one of them hadn't gone splat against the back of my head all those years ago who knows where I'd be. However, I will not thank Idiot Sir, bullies or dog poo; as the pusher of this pencil, I reserve the right to occasionally be selective.

I only used one of my HB pencils. I have three other HB pencils, but this one is my very favourite. It has my teeth marks on the end of it so that it stands out as my special one. Plus, it's a little bit shorter than the others now, even though I sharpened it as carefully as I could. I have, however, used all of my HBs to rule off this section, to cut it off. Goodbye car crash story. And good riddance!

———————————————

———————————————

———————————————

———————————————

FOUR HBs AND A LIST

These car crash things happened about five years ago. I was ten then, soon to turn eleven. I'm fifteen now. It's taken all that time for me to get around to writing about the most important year in my life. It's when things started to change, not that I knew it at the time. It's these changes I'm going to tell you about, put them down on paper so they make sense to me, stay real, stay permanent. Such a lot happened in that one year, so much changed. Maybe that's why it's taken me so long to get around to doing this, which is good in a way because time gives you a bit of perspective when you look at something from a distance. It's also good because I'm a better writer now. But even though I'm fifteen, it's still a huge, gigantic, monumental, mega-big task. How would you like to sit down, grab a pencil of your own personal preference, and write about all the stuff that happened to you over a year five years ago? You wouldn't like to; I know that for certain. But these things didn't happen to you and it wasn't your life that changed. And you probably don't have the need, not like I do.

So, that was the plan; write about the year where my world changed. Seemed simple enough at the outset. Until it came time to actually start. Turns out that making plans is the easy part. I'd written about the mandarin incident and Idiot Sir, but that now seemed easy compared to a whole year. I was stuck on two questions: Where to begin? What to include? It was becoming a bit of a nightmare, a real pain. There were times when I got cranky about the whole business. Frustrated. Almost chucked a few tantrums. In private, mind you. But I didn't because at fifteen I'm more grown up now. Close call, though. All my own fault, of course. If I was still ten or eleven I would have given up, plonked it in the too hard basket and problem solved. But things are different now. That's what maturity does to you.

I was stuck, not one word written. So I gave myself a deadline for starting, thought it'd force me to get a move on. For six days I'd tried to get started. Had given myself a week, that was my deadline, so time was almost up. Each day I picked up my special HB, the one with my friendly teeth marks on the end, the veteran from my "car crash" story. With my special pencil in hand, I'd get out the sketchbook Lisatoa had given me, beautiful white pages, and I'd try to start. First out I'd sit all calm and restful, a nice beaming smile just like mum's Lord Shiva statue. But nothing came and the paper stayed blank. I tried a different smile, crinkled my eyes and puffed out my cheeks, like mum's little Buddha picture, which was silly because he certainly doesn't look as though he's about to get down to some good hard work. So, I gave up the calm, smiling approach and tried to force a start, really gripped that pencil and clenched all my muscles from jaw to toes. Made some *ahhh grrrr* sounds. Bit stupid when I think about it. If my HB felt it was being throttled it still didn't cough up a single word. Six days and zero done! I remembered Saraswati, which was a relief because this was definitely a job for her. I started repeating her name, getting louder each time until I was yelling as loud as I could. I guess it sounded like a spoiled child's tantrum, so no wonder she refused to help me. I whispered an apology and asked her politely and kindly to help me out, but she must have still been upset by my yelling.

My two questions remained: Where to begin? What to include? "Maybe you need a book with lined pages," Lisatoa said, "like we have at school." I told him, in my superior know-it-all voice, that this wasn't a 'keep between the lines' kind of story, which I thought sounded pretty smart, creative even. Then I added, "And I'm not a 'keep between the lines' sort of person," which is true, but mostly not true. But Lisatoa wasn't listening; some of my best lines are wasted because people just don't pay attention. I picked up my HB pencil, gave it another quick bite to wake it up and in the sketchbook wrote, all in capitals, DEAR DIARY. As soon as I'd done it, I knew it was a terrible idea. Not one of my best lines. I should probably rethink my superior know-it-all attitude. Lisatoa leaned over to take a look at my first great words, laughed and left the room. I think he just picks the times when he wants to pay attention. Luckily I like my pencils, because I had the urge to snap one in half. Or maybe two, just to get it out of my system.

I went into the kitchen to find the little book mum makes notes in. It's where she has her shopping list of all the different ingredients she'll need to make our dinners. I wanted her to get me a rubber because DEAR DIARY just had to go. Apart from her shopping mum also has lists of books she wants to read, letters to be written, phone calls to be made and bills to pay. Mum uses a 2B pencil. Each to their own, I say. And mum always gets through her lists, gets the jobs done, the lists seem to work.

If I was a cartoon character, this would be when a big lightbulb next to my head lights up. Or maybe shooting stars could come out of my eyes and ears. Or pearls and gems could flow like a glittering river out of my nose. I think I'll probably rub out that last one.

So, that was it, I'd start with a list, it'd get me rolling. "Get ready special HB," I yelled, "because we are rolling to lift-off and it's full steam ahead!"

The bush is on the list. There's a River God. An exploding truck. A missing hand. And leg too, I suppose. A wooden statue, that mightn't really be a statue. There are a dead dad's diaries in a hidden cave. Spartacus, Snarkey and the hippies. There's Clarry and the gnomes. There's how to grow a hand and other magics. Though magic mightn't be the right word, but it'll have to do for the time being because I am now on a roll and will not be distracted! Except... except, I think I've had enough of list making... there's more, a whole lot more but I get the feeling I could be here forever just making a list. Let's just assume that I've rolled and rolled and now have lift-off. Plus, this list making could get a bit boring if I'm honest. And if I'm bored, then you must be too.

Sorry. Not a good way to set out. Sorry. But could you trust me, just a little trust? I think it's like when mum gets out all the ingredients she'll need to make our dinner. She lines them up in the order she'll use them. My mum is very organised and methodical, much more than I am, though I have been making my bed, tidying my room and packing my school bag all on my own over the last six days. Though it's possible that that's got something to do with avoiding facing the blank pages of the sketchbook Lisatoa gave me. If you saw all the things mum has lined up on our kitchen bench, no way would you ever believe it would make a delicious meal. You'd just see some potatoes and onions (boring) and a jumble of spices and herbs, like chilli powder, cumin, paprika, coriander, fenugreek and garlic (bit unusual). You'd think all these things couldn't come together to make a yummy yummy dinner, but you'd be wrong if you sat down and shared our Rajasthani onion and potato curry.

My list is like all the ingredients mum lines up for our dinner, they look like they could never come together to make something. But I'm going to take each ingredient on my list, prepare and cook it, so that I can explain how things happened, how things changed me, how I came to be not missing a single thing. So, like I said, give me a bit of trust; wait till you taste my Rajasthani onion and potato curry!

I'm a bit pleased with myself, the list has done the trick, got me rolling to lift-off. And it feels good. If an HB pencil can feel happy and satisfied, then I know my one does. I reckon I might even use all of my HB pencils, let them all have a turn.

I wasn't at all sure if Saraswati had anything to do with getting me started, but thanked her nevertheless; best to play it safe with a goddess who can be a little touchy.

Oh, and I mustn't forget to introduce myself. Everyone calls me Ray.

I'm giving what I'm doing a special name. Got to emphasise its importance. I'm calling it MY PROJECT and it's the biggest I have ever taken on. My capital letters, a nice touch I think, should make that pretty clear.

Look, I know it's not too promising when I recall those other projects I'd started but never finished. No capitals for those ones, you'll notice. But in my defence I always had excellent reasons for not completing those other ones. For example, I would have continued writing in my journal every single day if I hadn't lost it somewhere in my bedroom. And the man at the aged care home I'd volunteered to read to every Saturday morning never listened to *Winnie the Pooh* and spent his time either pretending to be asleep, swearing, picking his nose or telling me to duck down the road and grab him a beer. So, no point in keeping that up. And with the thousand-piece jigsaw puzzle of the Taj Mahal that I stupidly bought, I don't think all the pieces were there. This PROJECT will be different. Promise. I've already had a bit of practice with writing lots of stuff, starting with my sea-faring adventure stories (that weren't really about sea-faring adventures) that I did ages ago. I've got high hopes for this PROJECT. It's important to me.

I'm starting with the bush; it's top on my list and a good place to begin.

I wandered into the bush the very first day we moved here. That was five years ago, but I remember it clearly. It's like a little movie in my head that starts out all slow in black and white but ends up fast and full of colours. There was the removal truck parked across the front lawn, a portable radio sitting on its bonnet babbling talkback shows. Big men in sweaty singlets unloading furniture, drinking beer at lunch. The endless unpacking of cardboard boxes, the tired shuffling of my feet. A faded blue loungeroom carpet, islanded with so many things yet to find their place. A house of strange rooms still holding the marks and smells of others just moved out. I stepped outside into a late afternoon, the sky darkening to a bruised blue, birdsong slowly fading. A warm breeze carried the muffled sounds of distant cars, a radio, someone arguing and the sad howling of some lonely dog. I stood on the back verandah, my mind stuck on the dread of starting school the next day. I hated starting a new school, just hated it. I hated schools, full stop! But you already know that. I thought exploring the bush beside the river might take my mind off tomorrow. Worth a try.

As I moved deeper into the bush, night-time darkness quickened by the tall trees, I could hear the smooth murmur of the nearby river. I wound my way between thick-trunked gums, running my hand along their bark. A shift in the breeze and the giant trees rustled and groaned. I pushed aside low growing tea-trees and breathed in memories of colds and soothing ointments. Came upon a narrow dirt road, pot-holed and rutted either side of a long, raised strip of tufted grass. I turned right, planned to head towards the river, find a spot, take a seat and try to think about anything but school. I wished I could meditate like mum can; the crossed leg bit is super easy for me, but the hands in prayer position is just impossible.

A short distance along the dirt road I could see a clearing, a half-circle right beside the river. A widening path of milky light jerked and wobbled in the dark. Someone with a torch. Surrounding trees huddled round and glowered down. An early moon, near full, glinted on the river, made flickering shadows in the bush. I crept a little closer and heard the splash and gurgle of something being tipped into the river. A gust of wind, leaves whiplashed and a large branch shifted enough for moonlight to show a man, stooped and wiry, carrying a container from the back of a small truck before placing it beside the river. He wore a wide-brimmed hat, dark shadow hiding his features. The side of his truck read *Snarkeys Garidge and Machanical*, the writing as poor as the spelling.

Another gust of wind, this one stronger still, and the man's hat was blown off. He dropped whatever he was carrying and hurried after it. A bald man, a jerky runner, blackened hands grasping for his hat. Above the sound of the wind, a groaning-growling noise came from one of the trees, then a loud cracking as one of the large branches snapped and fell onto the back of the truck. There was the sound of things being crushed and broken, then everything was still and silent, like a deep breath held. A small flame appeared in the back of the truck, squirming and wriggling as if trying to escape the branch that pinned it down. The bald man stopped chasing his hat and turned to stare. He then ran towards his truck where the fire, no longer squirming to be free, was dancing and flickering up the side of one of the crushed containers where black liquid glistened and trickled onto the ground.

The bald man didn't make it too much closer to the truck before there was a huge explosion, a tremendous *whump* sound as the truck was briefly lifted off the ground, all four wheels at once, like some startled cat that leaps upwards to land all hackles raised. Even from my distance at the edge of the clearing I still felt a wave of hot air wash over me, shaking all the leaves, leaving me feeling as if I'd stood too long and too close to some cracker night bonfire. The truck was completely engulfed in twisting, leaping flames. The bald man would be left with nothing more than a burnt-out shell, nothing to be salvaged. The fire then lost its energy and enthusiasm and settled into the methodical task of burning whatever was left. In the stuttering light of the fire the bald man seemed to be dancing about, kicking his legs and thrashing his arms, yelling all sorts of threats and swear words, until like the fire he ran out of energy and enthusiasm. When he started to scan the bush surrounding him, I thought it would be a good time to melt back the way I had come.

I hadn't gone too far when I saw two figures standing on a small rise off to my left. They stood stock-still, frozen in the moment of their surprise. In the dappled moonlight I could see that one of them was huge, tall and wide-shouldered. He just stood there, staring hard, maybe wondering what to do. He wore long pants, but was bare-chested, his entire upper body filled with the mesmerising curves and swirls of strange paintings, bright yellows and oranges, dark blues, slashes of red. He then broke eye contact with me, making me feel as if I'd just been released. He turned and began to move away. The other figure was much smaller, shorter, but still with the suggestion that there was strength in that body. Before also moving away the smaller figure paused and gave me what might have been a smirk or grimace, or possibly a friendly grin. He then held up a finger to his lips, and though I couldn't hear it, I know he told me shush, told me to keep quiet.

Walking home, I didn't give too much thought to starting school the next day.

I like to believe in omens, though I'm not sure that I really do. Mum's the same, though she calls them shakunam. But if I did believe in omens there was certainly plenty to be read into what happened that night beside the river.

But what happened beside the river that night didn't save me; morning came and school was just down the road waiting for me, ready to make me feel awkward and nervous, ready to make fun of me, make me feel odd and out of place.

This was my third school in five years, which I know doesn't sound too much; lots of kids have to go to different schools. I have mentioned (can't emphasise it enough) how I hated school, but it was always the first days that were the worst. There were the jokes at the start: "Bet you can't do pushups." "You got a hook for that, like in *Peter Pan*?" "Can I give you a hand there, new kid?"

Then there's sport. I'm a fast runner, but no one cares about that. I can't play rugby league or cricket, so that's always a big negative. I did give cricket a go once, but when I took a swing the bat flew out of my hand and whacked the boy in slips. However, I'm really good at soccer and have excellent dribbling skills and people can't often take the ball off me. But soccer isn't popular, just something teachers made you play on the asphalt playground at lunch times. Even then everyone thought it hilarious to make me play in goal. Then there was that first day when the kid beside me pretended to get something from under my desk and undid my shoelaces when she was there. I had to get Sir to do them up, because it was something I couldn't do on my own. I still remember Sir being annoyed, telling me his class wasn't kindy, and the whole class snickering behind my back. (Yes, that's the same Sir my mum slapped: Sir the idiot!)

I tried not to let any of this bother me too much, but there really wasn't any way to do that. I should know. Sometimes, I'd get home and stand in front of the mirror with my arms behind my back. Another time, trying hard not to think about who it had belonged to, I'd put on this old jumper that was way too big for me, and pull the sleeves down beyond where any hands would be. Mum's gardening gloves were the best and the worst. I'd first fit the left glove over the end of my left arm, then wriggle the fingers of my right hand into the other glove. In the mirror it looked wonderful, if tricking me to think something looked normal could be called wonderful. For a moment, a split second, it looked okay, but then the left glove slid off. Like I said, the gardening gloves were the best and the worst.

JUST NO ESCAPING IT

Mum walked with me to school that first day. My dad didn't come along because he was at work, but... Oh, look, I might as well get the bit about my dad out of the way. I didn't live with my dad, hadn't for years. He ran away and got another life. There, that's it. Well, almost. He used to send me postcards, like he was on some happy holiday and wanted to tell me what nice places he was seeing and how he was having a good time and lots of other stuff I couldn't understand. If I got one of his postcards I wouldn't read it right away, I thought he could wait till I was good and ready. I could be a tough guy when I had to be. I wouldn't read them at home, in case mum saw me looking at them, not because she might see what was written in them, she could easily do that before giving them to me; I didn't want her to see how I'd react in case she mistook my behaviour for caring about what he'd written. So, I'd take them somewhere private. Later, when we were here, it'd always be the bush. Not that the bush is some magic place, at least not in the sense that most people would use that word, but it can calm things down and make you feel better. And maybe that is a kind of magic. I'd sit on some sun-warmed sandstone rock, take out his postcard and read and re-read it until I thought I could look at it without feeling too much. There were times when I wished he'd stop sending them, they didn't fill the gap, they just made it bigger. In the beginning the cards had pretty pictures of some place in India, or Burma, Madagascar or Africa, but that wasn't the point. I used to think he sent the cards to make himself feel better, like some big man travelling around, and to make mum and me feel jealous. And if he had to send postcards I wished he wouldn't write so much on them, small writing all scrunched up, because what he said just didn't make sense. I think that's more than enough about my dad, because I'm still trying to get it completely straight in my mind, I'm working on it. I keep all his postcards, because they're like this invisible bridge between us and maybe it's possible that one day, ages and ages and ages from now, I'll cross that bridge, maybe meet him in the middle. Who knows, eh, who knows?

So, it was mum walking me to school that first day. It is not a good way to start a new school no matter how old you are. At least she didn't try to hold my hand. I told her I was fine, absolutely fine, to go on my own. "Of course, Krishna knows why I'm doing this, can't think of any reason at all," mum said in this exaggerated voice. She then pointed out that I'd not turned up on the first day at the previous two schools. Fair enough. Actually, it was almost the first week at the last school, but it didn't seem necessary to remind her. Mum stopped a block away from the front of the school and I was thankful for the small mercy. It wasn't that she trusted me, because she stayed there staring until I went in. She then waited until the bell, making certain the "went in" didn't quickly become "came out". I know this because I watched her watching.

While I was watching the watcher, I was waiting for it to start, waiting for a rerun of all those other first days. It was inevitable, like that French lady must have felt waiting for the guillotine to fall; just no escaping it. Not that it's all over and done with on the first day, it goes on and on. Death by a thousand cuts. That's an expression I'd overheard mum use once when she was talking to my dad.

I could hear kids yelling, screaming and talking, sounds of people running, balls being kicked and bounced, an argument, some kid crying, the raised voice of a teacher. Unfriendly sounds, rough and abrasive, all threatening me with things to come.

And it did start, the guillotine was falling. "Hey, new kid, yeah you, can I give you a hand there?" I'd heard it a hundred times before, but it still stung; just because someone's been punched a hundred times doesn't mean they don't still hurt and bruise. The kid was still laughing, thought himself so funny, when a girl came up beside him, stared him in the eye and said, "Yeah, and maybe he could give you a brain, big mouth." The girl then winked at me. I remember it clearly because as far as I know that was the first time anyone had ever winked at me. Quite nice, really. Besides, I'd take anything half friendly on a first day. Yeah, I know, no big deal, but I remember that wink as if it were something important. The girl then walked off. She had long black hair that was very shiny. It took me three days to find out that her name was Gina Fontana. As soon as she'd left, another kid came up to me, pointed and asked, "How'd that happen? Some horrible accident? Like with an axe or something? A sword?" When I told him I was born that way, he thought about it for a moment then told me that it'd be even worse if I was left-handed. I didn't have an answer to that, so he lost interest and left. It was a new one on me. When some little kid, first or second class, stood in front of me with one of his books open and asked if I could do his maths homework for him, I had to give him the bad news that I was terrible at maths. "Thanks for nothing you dope. You probably can't count to ten anyway," he told me as he left. Two girls came up to me and started making strange movements with their hands. When I asked, "What are you doing?" one of them gave a startled, squeaking sound and said, "Wow! We didn't think you could talk. But you can! English too!" Then there was this tall kid, bright red curly hair, who came up to me and sang, yes, he sang to me, "Hey there, newish kid, standin' in the school so fancy free." He stopped there and took a small bow and said, "That's sorta from Georgy Girl, that song by the Seekers. I'm going to be a singer like Frank Sinatra." He then took a long look at me and said, "Oh, that's a pity. I could use a pi-ano player. My name's Kevin." He then walked off. I remember thinking his singing was pretty good. Only later did I realise that this was a good omen, a good shakunam, because I was thinking about someone's singing, my mind not completely full of fear for what lay ahead.

There was other stuff, but that was pretty much it. I didn't feel completely good about it all, but then again I didn't feel completely bad about it. At least not as bad as I was expecting. Perhaps, I'd gotten that little bit tougher. Or more likely it was because a couple of nice things happened that first day. There was the dark-haired girl who told someone he needed a brain, and there was that wink she gave me. And when we went into class there was this kid who smiled, pointed to an empty desk, waving his hand to tell me take a seat. Plus, the musical introduction from Kevin. And there was Stephan, who could be a little crazy, who sat with me that first lunch time. It looked like I had escaped the falling guillotine.

So, all things considered, it wasn't a bad start for me. I congratulated myself for turning up on my first day.

Writing all this has taken me a whole eleven days. Glad I didn't snap my HB in half, like I felt back at the start. I might even have apologised to my HB. Us writers do such crazy things. That is the first time I have called myself a writer, but I like the sound of it, it's my little reward for HBing all those words down. I am a writer, writer, writer! Though I don't think I'm ready to say it out aloud yet. So far I've had to sharpen my pencil three times and I calculate that it's used up about one eighth of my pencil. It looks like I will definitely need to call on my other HBs, though I think one sketchbook should do the trick. My list idea, borrowed from mum, has got the ball rolling. Time to pat myself on the back. Well done Ray, hurray!

I like writing, it's what I'm best at. It's something I can do on my own and if I don't want anyone to see what I've written, I just keep it hidden. Now that I'm fifteen and in high school it's my best subject. When I turned fifteen I won the writing competition run by our local library. I even write a school report for every Parents and Citizens letter the school sends out; the principal is very grateful because he says he has better things to do. But back when I was eleven I didn't willingly show anyone a single word of what I was writing; if I had to do some writing in class I'd write really boring stuff, just like everyone else was doing. I tried to be invisible back then, a little nothing hiding at his desk, but of course it never really worked. Don't have to do that anymore; I like showing my writing because some people think it's okay and that makes me feel proud. Everyone should feel proud about at least one thing they do, and writing is my one thing. I'm much, much better at writing than I am at maths.

I'm getting the feeling that this PROJECT is going to be even bigger than I thought at the start. But I'm going to keep at it. It's not going to be like that thousand-piece jigsaw puzzle, which if I'm honest might very well have had all the pieces. And, okay, I could have easily found my journal; my bedroom isn't that big. While I'm being honest, I have to tell you that what I write gets shown to someone else. Miss was someone who helped me a real lot. She was the first person to help me with MY PROJECT. Whilst I'm pretty good at writing, what I do isn't perfect and I make tons and tons of mistakes. Mind you, when my HB is flying across the page I think every word is perfect and brilliant. At first, I felt bad getting help, like it wasn't my writing anymore, but Miss said all writers have editors and they show their work to as many people as possible. "Writers always get help. Even Shakespeare, I imagine," she said. I was convinced, quite easily really, probably because I really am a writer. Later I showed MY PROJECT, my writing, to other people and it was always helpful. But no matter how much they all helped me, how much they polished, shined, cut and corrected, in the end the writing was still mine and only mine. They just made the telling clearer.

Miss' full name is Dorothea Windsor and she was my year six teacher when I was eleven. She is the best teacher I've ever had.

She's also one of the best people I've ever known, which puts her a zillion, trillion miles ahead of Idiot Sir with his photos of Surf Lifesavers; I bet he can't even swim, probably allergic to sand. Miss went overseas for a while, but she came back. She lives nearby, so I get to see her quite often. I am allowed to knock on her door if I need to talk or show her my writing. How special is that! I still call her Miss. I learnt Miss' full name when I saw it written in big swirly letters on the top of her class roll. I was standing beside her desk getting my Maths homework corrected when the principal, Mr Jones, came into our class. He told me to stand back while he talked to Miss. Don't know why he bothered, because I could still hear, along with the rest of the class. Mr Jones was a little deaf, so he always spoke really loudly; good for assemblies, bad for private conversations. Perhaps he thought everyone else was a little deaf too. Mr Jones had a great deal of hair growing out of his ears, but I don't think anyone ever pointed out the possible connection. As he was leaving, Mr Jones told Miss that she should remove her name from the front of her roll "because it just doesn't do for the students to know your Christian name, doesn't do at all." He paused a moment, seemed to hesitate, then added, "Nor does it do for lady staff members to be wearing trousers, or slacks if you will. Trousers for men; skirts or dresses for the ladies." When he left the room, I heard Miss under her breath say, "This is 1966, not 1866." Miss wore trousers every day for the rest of the week. The clothes Miss wears are different to my mum's, but I still like how she dresses, especially her shirts with their patterns of brightly coloured flowers. It was like a little bit of a garden came into our class when she wore them. If a lady wears trousers or a shirt, they're supposed to be called slacks or blouse: how stupid is that? I never told people that I liked the shirts Miss wore. But I have now!

After surviving my first day at school, things seemed to cruise along pretty smoothly. In terms of school I'm a big fan of things cruising along smoothly. It was even full steam ahead some days. So, I don't know why I had to rock the boat. All right, all right I'll stop the nautical imagery; I was just flexing my writing style muscles, building them up, it's what us writers do. In the end it was me who caused the problem. I don't really want to tell you some of the stuff in this next bit, but Miss says, "Writers should never shy away from the truth." And I hadn't even told her I was a writer! It must just show. I ignored Miss' advice for a while. Us writers should get to pick and choose, I told myself. But I didn't believe it. Besides, I already told you about hating school, before the one with Miss, and I told you about my dad, and about the bullying, and the sock puppet incident, and the mandarin-dog poo-no pants tragedy.

I have to tell you about the slapping; it's another bad thing from which some good things came. I'd been at the school for almost a month, so there's no way I could claim ignorance. At eleven I should have known better. It's like, if you know a dog is really aggressive, been made that way by some nasty, dumb owner, then you don't go poking and irritating it because there's a good chance it just might up and bite you. I knew Alex was like a big dog that had somehow got made bad and angry. So, no excuses.

It was lunch time and Alex was sitting in the corner of the playground with his back against the trunk of a peppercorn tree. He was eating his lunch, a large packet of hot chips that he got from the fish and chip shop down the road. You weren't allowed to leave school grounds at lunch, but each day Alex would go to the chip shop and come back and sit against the peppercorn tree, his tree. This particular day, the day of slapping, I was walking past Alex and his bag of chips and... well, they smelled delicious. I've always liked chips. Still do, though it's not what we have at home.

Whenever Alex sat against his peppercorn tree, eating his chips, there'd be this invisible circle around him that no one entered. Everyone understood that this zone was a no-go one. It was as if Alex was leashed to his tree by some unseen chain that allowed him to circle his tree and it would be silly if someone were to stumble into that circle. I don't think I ever saw a teacher enter that forbidden circle, except when Alex wasn't there and they'd go in to pick up the lunch rubbish he always left behind. So, don't ask me how I got inside the forbidden circle, but there I was, reaching into Alex's packet of chips. It wasn't even one of the really fat chips that came away in my hand, which looking back makes the whole thing just that bit more pathetic. And I didn't even get to eat that lousy chip, because Alex jumped up and slapped it out of my hand. He then slapped my face. Yes! He slapped my face! It was a while ago now, but I think I can still hear the sharp crack of that slap and I remember the shock I felt at the force and anger behind it. It should have been my face that was hurting most, and I guess it was, but it was my stomach that got my attention, a stomach that felt like it was dissolving, as if everything inside was melting into some nasty liquid. All I could think was to hope not too many people were watching and that I would not go to the toilet in my pants, please don't go to the toilet in my pants. Some things are a lot harder to get over than others, and I think there's general agreement that pooing your pants in the middle of the playground is right up there at the top. Alex then slapped me again, and I felt my world collapsing in upon me. I'd stuck up my good arm, but he just slapped through it. Alex then leant in close to my face, and hissing through clenched teeth told me, "Soldiers die of cigarette bullets." I think Alex might have been about to hit me again, but I got rescued. Someone came up from behind me. I like to think there was a brief shadow passing over me as that someone came up beside me, but that's most un- likely, shade of the peppercorn tree and all that. A large arm went out and grabbed Alex's swinging wrist. "Stop. Now!" was all that was said, and it worked because Alex stopped slapping and sat back down to finish his chips. It was Lisatoa, and at that time those two words were the most I had ever heard him speak. I was about to say something, mumble a thank you, but he held a finger to his lips, telling me to shush. A smirk that turned into a friendly grin told me where it was that I had first seen him. I then tossed my head back and gave a loud "Ha, ha, ha," (Krishna knows why!) and walked off slowly in the direction of the toilets, because I figured that's how a cool, calm and unruffled person would move, but about halfway there I needed to break into a run. Oh, well. I made it in time. Just. Of course there was no toilet paper and I had to use my hanky, but at least no one could see that.

I know that us writers should embrace as wide a range of experiences as possible, so that it will enrich our writing. But I can tell you, there was zero embracing on my part. My writing doesn't need face slapping to be enriched, thank you very much. It's like that stupid saying Idiot Sir used to repeat every second day: "Whatever doesn't kill you makes you stronger." What rubbish! So, I'm supposed to believe that one Monday Idiot Sir would come into whatever unlucky class he had and tell them that, "While rescuing thousands of people from tsunami size surf I was attacked by a shark that ate both my legs and both my arms. But I'd like to thank that wonderful shark because I feel much stronger now!"

Again, I knocked on the door to Miss' house and asked her to take a look at what I'd written. Along with suggestions (a few) and corrections (plenty) Miss said, "You certainly didn't shy away from the truth." Handing my writing back she added, "Do you wonder if you'd politely asked Alex if you could have one of his chips, swap it for a drink or something, it could have turned out differently? You just never know." If Miss had said that to me five years ago, I'd have thought her a bit crazy, totally unrealistic. I'd have thought she doesn't understand a thing about Alex. But I would have been wrong.

As I was looking over the suggestions and corrections, I noticed I'd written "I stuck up my good arm" to try and stop Alex. *Good* arm! I'm not going to do that anymore because I don't think I've got one good arm and one bad arm. I don't have a *bad* arm; I have an arm that's different, an arm that's a bit of a disability, an arm that makes people stare and ask silly questions. But I don't have one good arm and one bad arm. So there.

Since Lisatoa was sort of the hero in this last bit of writing, I asked him if he'd also read it over. He did give it a go, but he wasn't all that helpful. Okay, in fact he was hopeless, just kept saying, "Perfect. Yep, brilliant." Even suggested I use a biro! A biro! He'd probably tell Rembrandt to use textas. However, he did offer to do some drawings; illustrations, I'm supposed to call them, though I really can't see the difference. At first, I thought that might be a good idea, see how it turns out, lots of great books have illustrations. He said he wasn't very good at doing people yet, but would do his best to capture the action of me getting slapped and slapped by Alex. I decided that MY PROJECT really didn't need any illustrations, lots of great books don't, and told him to hold off for the time being.

A QUICK PEEK INTO 6W

I don't want to give you the idea that the slapping was just one of the many miserable things that happened to me at that school. Nor do I want you to think that everything else was all happy and wonderful. My maturity, my fifteen years of experience, tells me that things just don't work out like that; most times things are a bit of a mixture. And a mixture I could handle. Idiot Sir's class wasn't a mixture. Maybe if I take you inside my classroom, get you to meet some of the people, look at some of the stuff that went on, that might be best.

My class was 6W, room 11. It became the best class I had ever been in. I was moving on from being a school hater. Our classroom was all on its own, away from the rest of the school, which is exactly how it should have been because we were the only year six class. It would have been nice if our classroom had been on the top of a small hill, so that we could look down at the rest of the school. But you can't have everything. Our room used to be two classrooms joined together, so there was tons of space for Mr Jones to stack the school's Duke of Edinburgh Award camping gear. Lisatoa had been at this school for five years and he said there had never ever been a camp, which he said was very disappointing for everyone. Though I don't think that included the Duke. Or me. Went camping with my dad five times and it was really great fun. So, I didn't want to go camping again. Just yet. Miss hated the camping gear in her room, but I think she left it there out of respect for the Duke. The Duke lives in London, which meant Miss would have a soft spot for him. Miss was a tiny bit keen on London and things British. That last sentence is the writer in me using the technique of understatement.

Our classroom had these big wooden windows that were excellent for staring out of, though only a couple of them could be opened, which in summer was not so excellent. Alex used to

30

squash blowflies against the window nearest him. I even heard them crunch a couple of times. Miss would get him to wipe the window clean with one of the small towels from the Duke of Edinburgh camping gear and to then put it in the bin. She never told Alex off. Perhaps it was part of Miss' plan to be rid of the camping gear one small piece at a time. Our classroom had the biggest and best blackboard in the whole school, even though some of its corners were broken off. Some sections were really shiny and Miss couldn't write on them. One time, just to make conversation, I told Gina Fontana we had the biggest and best blackboard. For a moment, I thought she wasn't interested in my making conversation, but then she said, "How's that?" So, I told her how it was wider than any of the others. "Yes, yes," she said, "but why the best?" Just then Kevin was walking past and I wanted to ask how his singing was going, so I had to excuse myself. It would have been a whole lot easier if Gina had just smiled and nodded her head at my blackboard conversation starter, perhaps adding something about what lovely windows we had. Oh, well.

I used to sit at the back of the room, one desk in front of Alex, but decided to move in order to improve my education. I remember telling Miss the blackboard was a little hard for me to see from where I was seated. When she asked me why that was, I told her it was because I was farsighted, like mum said when she had to get glasses. Or mum might have said nearsighted. Doesn't matter because she never wore the glasses anyway. I think I just liked saying I was farsighted, it sounded as if I could peer into the future and cleverly plan ahead, and that'd be handy. Miss just gave me a smile that matched her lovely shirt and moved me to the desk beside Kevin, who didn't sing in class. But he did hum a lot, which could be soothing at times and annoying at others. I didn't move back to my old desk, however. Give me humming over the crunching of blowflies any day.

Lisatoa sat in a corner of the room. He had two desks to himself, which was perfect for doing his drawings. Illustrations. Even then he was becoming something of an artist. Miss tended to leave Lisatoa alone to get on with whatever it was that he is getting on with. She probably thought he was working through her "stimulating and individually tailored syllabus". Besides, she had Alex in her class, and that had to be enough for any teacher. Every time I looked in Lisatoa's direction, or nonchalantly cruised past his desk, he was either looking through some book on art or writing and drawing in one of his sketchbooks. I remember the first time I saw his work, how neat and perfect it was, no smudges or scribblings, no crossings out. Some of his illustrations were fantastic, really detailed and colourful. His desktop was always organised, no chaotic mess, books in a tidy pile, his pen wiped clean and laid beside his inkwell. His bookwork was much better than anyone else in the class and it was certainly a zillion zillion miles better than Alex's; mum once showed me a picture in one of her too-heavy-to-hold books of something called the Rorschach test, which is exactly what Alex's books looked like. The Rorschach test is just a big blob of spilled ink that people are supposed to look at and say what it is that they think they can see. I can do that with clouds, so I don't know why Mr Rorschach got so famous for his inkblots.

The only time I remember Lisatoa paying close attention to anything that was going on in class was the time I had to read out my composition. It was during my first weeks at this school when Miss came up with "a light-bulb idea to get our creative juices flowing." So, each Friday afternoon we had "Create a Story Time", which was an hour and a half where you were supposed to work on your composition. Then about an hour before the end of class five pupils were picked to come and stand at the front of the class and "whisk us all away with the magic of words." Unfortunately, there were very few magic words and consequently very little whisking away. Mostly, kids would mumble their way through a bit of story ("Not finished yet, Miss."), then sit back down. Miss would then call out their mark, which couldn't have been easy for her because she rarely looked up from her London travel brochures (Friday was travel brochure day). She only paid attention if a story included something British in it, London preferably, which resulted in all sorts of strange and improbable stories. There was Gina's story which started out with her father bringing home a tiny ginger cat ("I really, truly love that felis catas, Miss.") that he'd found abandoned at his work one day. The tiny ginger cat and Gina became inseparable. One day it followed Gina to the beach and when Gina got caught in a rip it swam out and saved her. Gina then had to take her cat to Trafalgar Square where he was used as a model for the lion statues around Nelson's column. This all made for a very tiring day, so Gina was pleased to return to her castle in the very centre of London for some well-earned rest and lots of vino. Gina didn't get to finish her story, because she began laughing and couldn't seem to stop. Despite all this, Gina got a good mark, along with a strange look from Miss.

The only person who didn't get a good mark and who mentioned London was Alex who refused to come to the front of the classroom or to even stand up to read. His story was about the Great Fire of London and how it was started by a clever boy and his stolen cigarette lighter. Alex then started listing different buildings that got burnt: "The bakery burnt down, then the fruit shop burst into flames, big, big flames, then the milkbar owned by the man who called the cops on me exploded in giant flames, then the church and then our school and...". Alex's reading got faster and faster, his voice screeching higher and higher. It was then that Miss told Alex (three times) that he had to stop and that he should go outside and get a drink from the bubbler. As he was leaving, Alex paused at the door and yelled as loudly as he could, "But the jungle wouldn't burn, Miss. Burn jungle, burn! But it just wouldn't. I wished it had. I hate jungle, I hate cigarettes. Hate them." When he turned around I could see his eyes were wet and glistening. Probably from all that screaming I thought. The class stayed silent, waiting for Miss to do something about Alex's behaviour. But Miss didn't do a single thing.

At first I hated the idea of Create a Story Time, couldn't think of anything worse than standing in front of the class and speaking out aloud; everyone would be staring at me as I stood there, shaking hand trying to hold my book open and turn the pages. So for the first few weeks I wrote nothing. But Miss was having none of that and told me that if I didn't write something to be read out I would have to move back next to Alex because at least he was getting something done. It wasn't much of a choice. I picked the lesser of two evils and started to do some writing. When time for my story finally came around it turned out that I had a nine-page monster to read. It seemed like an awful lot of words for a school story, and I couldn't explain how I'd written that much, how all those blank pages came to be full of words. Now, looking back, it was obviously the beginning of my destiny to become a writer. That day in class must have been my first time to be "in the thrall of the muse". That's an expression Lisatoa's mum told me, saying it comes in handy when you have no idea what you're doing. Anyway, I had this gigantic story, so I decided to read a bit, then give Miss the "Not finished yet, Miss," line. But I don't know what happened there either, probably the muse again, because I ended up reading the whole thing. The story was about a boy whose family used to be very rich, but had lost everything and ended up in the slums of London (got to play the game). The boy lived with his mum who really loved him as much as she could. The boy, Tobias, spent his days on the docks of the Thames waiting for his dad to come back from being on one of Nelson's ships in the Battle of Trafalgar. One day he was mudlarking along the banks of the river when he found some very valuable Roman coins. Just then he saw his father's ship returning and it looked all damaged and shot up ("crippled and ravaged by deadly cannonballs"). When his father came ashore Tobias was horrified to see that his father only had one leg, the missing leg replaced by a wooden one. Tobias was about to burst into tears, but stopped when his father grinned widely and said, "Just like Long John Silver, eh? But I can't stay, I've got things to do. Here's a postcard for you." And with that Tobias' father turned around and walked away. Tobias was very glad he didn't show his dad the valuable Roman coins. Tobias went to wave goodbye to his dad, but realised his dad wasn't even looking. When Tobias got back home he didn't mention his father, because his mother knew all about that sort of thing. The last lines of my story were when Tobias showed his mother the valuable Roman coins, and she said, "Let's get away from here, let's have an adventure. We can buy a ship and we can go adventurin'!" When I read those last words I felt like I'd climbed this really high mountain, a little light-headed and breathing deeply, and looking down I could see all these obstacles I'd managed to overcome or avoid. For a moment I just stood there, until Miss got up from her desk and said, "Three hearty British cheers for Ray's story. That's ten out of ten, Ray. Top drawer!" I felt proud and happy about my story, big Cheshire-cat-grin happy, even when Miss said, "And in the ensuing weeks we can all look forward to Ray telling us more about the adventurin' Tobias and his mother get up to." I usually wrote my Friday story with pen and ink, but if I wanted to go really fast I used some 2B pencils. It was only later that I realised the error of my ways, matured as a writer, and settled on HB pencils.

I didn't get the three cheers that Miss asked the class to give, at least not hearty ones, but that was okay because I completely understood how jealousy is not a pleasant thing. Passing Gina's desk, she looked at me, friendly smile across her face, and told me, "Not bad, but rubbish compared to mine. And control that grin of yours, or the top of your head'll fall off." I didn't answer her, didn't fire off some witty and crushing response, because just then I saw Lisatoa looking up at me and nodding three or four times, before going back to whatever it was that he was doing in his book.

Later, as I was passing Lisatoa's desk, at pack up time that afternoon, he had out the book he did his drawings in. On a double page, in mesmerising writing of curves and swirls, were the words, "Good Story". I don't think I had ever felt so good about being in a classroom.

THE EVENTFUL ARRIVAL OF MR DODD AND HIS QUIET DEPARTURE

All in all, Friday "Create a Story Time" wasn't a bad way to end the week and I even started to look forward to it. It was certainly a lot better than Friday morning. Each Friday morning we had thirty minutes of Religious Instruction, which never resulted in anyone being instructed in anything to do with religion. At first Miss was happy that we were to have our thirty minutes of Religious Instruction because she didn't have to stay in the classroom and probably went off to organise her travel brochures while sipping a cup of tea. But she didn't get to do that for too long, because unless she stayed in the classroom Religious Instruction turned into a bit of a riot; a riot, I will admit, that was very funny and enjoyable. I know you shouldn't laugh at things that are at the expense of someone else, it's devilishly naughty, but I bet if you'd been there you would have found it great fun too. I heard the expression "devilishly naughty" in some old English movie where this white-haired character, who was supposed to be a writer, would finish typing a chapter, sit back and rub his hands together and say, "Oh my word, that is so devilishly naughty." So, since I too am a writer, who was being a bit naughty, I think the phrase fits perfectly. Plus, I like the sophisticated sound of it.

My mum often talked about someone having a mean streak, or a creative streak, or an aggressive streak. Different people seemed to have different streaks running through them, perhaps like a vein of gold or coal in the earth. I think my mum studied some psychology, or maybe philosophy or whatever, (but not geology) so she should be a bit expert on this streak business. It made me wonder if this devilish naughtiness of mine was a sign that my impending teenage years, only fourteen months away, were seeing me develop a bit of a larrikin streak. Whereas Alex was developing a hoodlum streak, Lisatoa an artistic streak and Kevin a musical streak. Gina already had a fully developed clever, cheeky, amusing streak and a nice wink and smile. Of course, I was also developing my creative and sensitive writer's streak. I bring up this streak business because it's a fascinating piece of psychology, or philosophy, that you might like to ponder on as you go through life meeting different people.

Our Religious Instruction teacher was one of tallest people I'd ever seen, so tall that when he walked he seemed to wobble as if it were a little difficult to maintain balance on such long legs. He wore shorts and long white socks, so those long legs really were something you couldn't miss. (By the way, there's no such thing as a tall streak.) His short-sleeved shirt had two buttons missing (hairy belly peeping out) and the points of the collar were turned up so that they looked like little wings trying to take flight. He was a young man who had started early on the process of going bald. He had very long side levers, mutton chops Miss called them, but they didn't make up for the thinness of hair on top. When he first arrived, Miss left the room straight away, telling him that it'd be best if he "took command from the very start". When he wobbled into the room the class was completely quiet and attentive. We wanted to know if he was enemy or prey. It doesn't pay for the class to rush in, assuming the new person is prey, because if you get it wrong you could end up being the prey and copping all that goes along with that. So, we watched and we waited, building evidence. He moved towards the blackboard, picked up a stick of chalk and turned his back on the class, the first suggestion that he could be prey. He tried to write on one of the shiny bits, but that failed. He moved along to the right and tried again, but broke the stick of chalk, then broke it again before giving up. He turned around to face the class, wobbled a little, and said, "Dodd. I'm Mr Dodd. Dodd." Stephan was the first to start in.

I didn't know all that much about Stephan, but it'll help if I at least give you what I knew at the time. If I begin by telling you that Stephan had to sit as far away from Alex as possible, and on his own, then that should head you in the right direction. Stephan is from Yugoslavia, but every time he told someone this, and he wasn't averse to doing it repeatedly, he'd say, "I am Stephan, at your service, and I am from Jugofsaliva. Oops, Yugoslavia I mean." He'd then bubble saliva at the corners of his mouth, until it slid down his chin. A most memorable introduction. The next thing about Stephan was that he was always calling out, never thinking before he said something. If he was a cowboy in one of those shows I watch, he would be the 'shoot first and ask stupid questions later' character. Miss would tell him, "Silence, Stephan, not a word," before the start of any lesson, something she'd repeat at different intervals, just like a good cowboy (to continue my cowboy imagery) might shoot a round from time to time into the bush, just to make sure the baddies didn't make any unexpected moves. The other thing about Stephan is that he had this thing about farting. I know this doesn't sound very appealing, but it does sort of fit in with someone who bubbled and dribbled saliva down their face. It's not that Stephan did actual farts, though that wasn't for lack of trying, he just liked making those sounds, pretend farts. Someone would sit down and Stephan would make one of his farting sounds, always different, selected from his seemingly inexhaustible repertoire. Someone bending over; fart sound. Someone coughing, someone stretching, laughing, someone leaving the classroom, all got their custom-made fart sound. Stephan never tired of any of this, could be relied upon each and every day. "Enough Stephan, enough breaking wind sounds. Enough fake flatulence!" Miss once screamed at him, and since Miss never raises her voice the whole class fell completely silent, which I suppose looked like a victory for Miss over Stephan. But then she sat down. Even I thought that a bit funny, which was yet another sign of my developing devilish naughtiness. Though I also saw Miss smile, and she had to be years beyond any devilish naughtiness. That's it, I think I've had enough of the sophisticated sound of that expression now; devilish naughtiness has lost its shine.

Related to Stephan's ability with sound effects was his taking every opportunity to replace a similar sounding word with the word fart. Our Maths book is called Smart Maths, which for Stephan became Fart Maths. Ditto for Art lessons etc, etc, but it was during Miss' preparation for the school athletics carnival that Stephan's rhyming skills reached their peak: "All runners must wait for the starting gun." Farting bum was his first double and, to date, his only one.

However, Stephan's fixation with farting wasn't the thing I remember most about him. We were doing the Romans in class, a brief period away from anything British. Miss was telling us about this slave who led a rebellion of slaves "against the cruel power of Rome" and when the slaves were defeated in a battle lots of prisoners were captured, "And a prisoner is something nobody would ever want to be because you were almost certain to be crucified," Miss told us. But this time the Roman leader, "some name I can't remember", said they could all escape crucifixion if they pointed out who their leader was, "then only their leader would be on the receiving end of cruel death". Someone in class asked what crucifixion was, something even I knew, though I'd never been to Sunday School, so Miss had to pause to give an explanation. However, I don't think "stuck on a wooden cross until you die" really covered it. Miss told us how none of the prisoners would give up their leader, so they all got crucified, which didn't make much sense to me. "Each prisoner would jump forward and say he was the leader, so that the Romans couldn't know who the real leader was." By this stage I had to bet that I wasn't the only one who wondered what the slave leader's name was. Maybe it was just another name Miss couldn't remember, it not being English sounding. But Miss had her reasons. "Each slave stood up and yelled, "I'm Spartacus ... I'm Spartacus ... I'm Spartacus ..." Stephan missed the first time Miss said Spartacus, but thereafter there was the instant echo, slightly distorted, "I'm Fartacus." Even though I thought it a little crazy that everyone had to die, I still liked the story, thought there was something almost heroic and moving in it. It didn't even bother me when I later saw the movie *Spartacus* and figured that that was where Miss got her history from. And I mustn't have been the only one in class who liked the story of Spartacus, because as Miss continued with the story, half the class kept yelling at Stephan to shut up. For days you could hear kids in the playground yelling, "I'm Spartacus." I think Spartacus must have had a heroic and tragic streak a mile wide. Later, I would like the story of Spartacus even more. And that would be what I'd remember most about Stephan.

It seems to have taken me a while to get back to Mr Dodd and how Stephan was the first to identify him as prey. I think I took a bit of time telling you about Stephan because despite all that I've said about him, which hasn't been all that positive and nice, I still think he was okay. Sure, that's partly because he was the class clown who provided comic relief, the kid who was a little weird and interesting, but it's also because I liked him. Not in any best friend sort of way, but I did like him and knew there was more to him than being the kid who made farting sounds. It was lunchtime on my very first day at school and I was sitting on my own, the new kid who's different. On that day, it was Stephan who came over and sat beside me; he didn't make a farting sound, but did tell me he was from Jugofsaliva, and dribbled. He talked a bit about his family and I told him about my mum. ("You're lucky," he said, "my dad still doesn't speak English, doesn't even try.") Stephan was the first person to talk to me that day, really talk, because I don't count comments or questions about my left arm. He sat beside me eating what I later found out was a cevapi and rye bread sandwich. He looked at my lunch and didn't even ask what it was. I hope that explains things. I have no idea what streak Stephan was developing, it's a bit of a puzzle.

Sorry, still don't seem to be back to Stephan and Mr Dodd. It's the muse again. I'll get back now. It was when Mr Dodd introduced himself to the class.

"Dodd. I'm Mr Dodd. Dodd," he said, and that was Stephan's cue.

"Did you say your name is Mr God? Boy oh boy, we really are special," Stephan called out, and before Mr Dodd could answer he added, "Shouldn't you have a big white beard, not just those silly sideburns?"

"No, no, don't be silly, let me explain. Dodd is my name. Let me try the chalk and board again. If at first you don't succeed, try again I always say," and as he bent down to pick up one of the pieces of broken chalk Stephan made a long and loud farting sound. Mr Dodd quickly stood up, wobbled a bit while looking around the classroom. Someone yelled out, "My dad wobbles like that on Saturdays." Mr Dodd ignored the comment and turned to walk towards the board, each slow step accompanied by a different farting sound: like I said, Stephan had a varied repertoire. Mr Dodd almost finished writing his name on the board when he once again broke the chalk; it was the last d that was incomplete, so that his name read Dodo. He was prey.

"Dodo's an interesting name, Sir. Like the bird, you know the dodo. Lovely pink bird, really long legs. Bit like you, Mr Dodo," someone from the front of the class said.

"That's a flamingo, you idiot," Gina called out.

"Dodd, my name's Dodd."

"Don't call me an idiot." The person at the front was now standing up, turning around to face Gina. "They're all birds, so it doesn't matter. A bird is a bird. They all fly. So, ha!"

Kevin put his hand up, waved it around, but Mr Dodd ignored him. However, Kevin had something to say, "It's quite interesting actually. Lots of our feathered friends can't fly. Kiwi, ostrich, emu... lots can't fly. But they can sing, and that's the most important thing. Their musical voices..."

"Enough," Mr Dodd said. But if he was hoping for quiet, he needed to yell loudly, bang his hand on the desk and look threatening, maybe flaring his nostrils and baring his teeth; but all we got was "enough" said more as a plea than a command. Mr Dodd then proceeded to hand out sheets of paper, three or four stapled together. There was the heading "Bible Stories: The Good Samaritan". Front page was a picture of this man lying on the ground with someone standing over him with their fists clenched. The man on the ground, handsome with a lovely white robe, was bleeding everywhere, but the blood was this lovely shiny pink colour and he was looking up and smiling, like he was having a really good time. The person standing was, I suppose, meant to look mean and horrible, but his scrunched-up face just made him look as if he needed to get to a toilet really quickly. Besides all this, the man on the ground was much bigger than the one standing over him, so much so that it made it hard to see how he was the one who ended up on the ground.

Despite Mr Dodd handing out those sheets, some in the class still found birds to be more interesting. "Why are dodos extinct?" Alex asked as he climbed on top of his desk. "Tell me that. God loves everything, that's what my nan says, God loves everything. So, how come he lets things die? How come he let all the dodos die? That's what I want to know, how come he lets things die? Things you love. How come?" The class was completely quiet. The way Alex had been talking, the words racing out, made him sound crazy. But he wasn't, I found out later. Or if he was, he had his reasons.

It was while the class remained quiet that Kevin seized his opportunity, stood up and said, "I think I can help you, Sir, get the class in the religious mood." He then began to sing "Silent Night", which sounded a bit Christmassy for July, though it was a very nice version and the class did stay quiet. As Kevin was finishing

Gina stood up and started to applaud. "Encore Kevin, encore!" she cried. Some others joined in. Stephan shrieked a loud whistle, a novel wind noise for him. Kevin was grinning, took a bow, then started singing "Jingle Bells".

"Thank you, Kevin, enough. Enough!" It was Miss at the door, pointing one of her rolled up travel brochures at Kevin, who sat down, show over. Miss might have been a small person, but she had some sort of power about her, and when she wanted to use it it was pretty hard to ignore. There was this energy about her. When she walked across the playground, her blonde hair bobbing up and down and swinging from side to side, it was a sure sign of that energy bubbling away. So, no surprise that when Miss said "enough" it packed a lot more punch than Mr Dodd's. "Everything all right in here, Mr Dodd?" It must have been what Miss called a rhetorical question, a question that someone asks even though it doesn't need an answer, which seems a little pointless if you ask me. "Alex, off your desk. Now, Alex, now!" Miss then looked at the writing on the board. "Sorry, I thought you said your name was Dodd." It was then that the whole class burst into laughter. And there I was, laughing as happily and loudly as any of the others, no longer a little nothing hiding at his desk.

For the rest of that lesson we had to copy into our books all the writing that was in the stapled papers that we'd been given. Lisatoa included the picture in his and, of course, it was ten times better than the one we'd been given.

We only had two more Religious Instruction lessons with Mr Dodd; he just stopped turning up, quietly disappeared. Perhaps because he was most definitely prey, (victim streak) but I suspect it was mainly because Miss never really got to escape with her travel brochures and had to keep coming back to class to settle things down. Gina said Mr Dodd had chosen to go to the Congo to be a missionary in preference.

Sometimes, instead of Religious Instruction, Miss would take us out to the school Memorial Garden where there was a plaque with the names and ages of some ex-students who had been killed in the First World War. Alex always refused to go with us and simply sat down on the steps that led into our classroom. And all Miss said to him was, "That's fine Alex, take your time." It wasn't much of a memorial, everything weedy and overgrown. Miss got us to weed and tidy up the garden and it did start to look a lot better, bit like a proper garden. The next week Miss brought in a small tree in a pot. "An English oak, ordered in from Tasmania. Live for hundreds and hundreds of years," Miss said. "Grow big and strong, just like things should. The right thing for here." And in a strange way Miss was right, because I saw that two of the boys had been killed when they were just eighteen.

Apart from the times we went to the Memorial Garden, each Friday morning was spent copying out huge slabs of writing from some Church of England booklets. Kevin asked if we could sing hymns, make a choir with him being the lead singer. Miss looked around the room, laughed and shook her head. So, we were stuck copying out those booklets. I reckon half the class wasn't Church of England. I know I wasn't. I'm still not decided yet, but I fancy mum's "set of beliefs".

LET ME TELL YOU A BIT MORE ABOUT LISATOA

If I had to pick one big, main, central, most important reason why things changed for me over that year then that reason would be Lisatoa. That's why I'm going to give you a bit of a closer look.

Where the bush starts, not too far from the back of my house, all the plants and trees are crushed and broken where people have backed their trailers and utes in to dump rubbish, which could be anything from grass cuttings to empty beer bottles, smashed furniture, car batteries, old tyres, cracked pieces of fibro and kitchen garbage. It's ugly and it stinks; only droning blowflies and scurrying rats stay longer than necessary. The local tip is nearby, but they charge for taking your rubbish, and even if it was the smallest possible amount people still dumped their rubbish because adults can sometimes be mean and stupid. Usually, the men. I bet no writer would drive there to dump their rubbish; writers make beautiful things, they don't make and dump garbage. (The writing on postcards doesn't count; nor do my early scribblings, because that was before the muse and I hit it off.) There's a good side to the rubbish though. Mum often says: "Every cloud has a silver lining."

The silver lining in the cloud of the rubbish is that it keeps lots of people away, stops them going further into the bush and getting to where the National Park begins. I just know that if they started going there they would end up wrecking it too. It's like the beautiful bush is hiding behind all the rubbish, telling people, "No, no don't come in here, it's just more filthy rubbish, best stay away." And it works, the rubbish keeps them away, which meant that deeper into the bush could be my place, my magic escape, one that for a long time I didn't have to share.

When mum and I first arrived here the bush was my hiding place, my safe place. In the bush I didn't have to control my feelings; nobody could see or hear me there. Later I would share the bush, but by then that was just fine. In fact, by then it was exactly what I wanted. I knew I wasn't the first to appreciate this place; I'd found plenty of evidence for that in some of the caves. That there'd been people before me made me feel as if I was part of something bigger, more than I could ever comprehend, and that sometimes you just have to accept what you don't fully understand. Like how it came about that I got sent postcards.

It was after my chip and slap run-in with Alex that it first came about that I would share the bush. I needed to wander into the bush, find one of my spots and just sit there and let everything settle down. When I was deep in the bush, the deeper the better, any bad stuff that had happened didn't seem so bad. I remember how my heading into the bush started to work straight away, taking my mind off being slapped right in the middle of the playground. I began thinking about other stuff, like *Bonanza*, one of my favourite cowboy shows. Previews for that night's episode showed the goodies sitting around their campfire when some mean looking hombres wander in and you just know that that means trouble is a brewin' and pearl-handled six-shooters will be called upon. I was looking forward to that episode. I thought that if I was a cowboy I would spend most of the time all on my own, just me and my friendly horse. I once told mum I wanted to be a cowboy, even though I'd be hopeless at riding a horse. She screwed up her face and tilted her head sideways, but broke into a smile when I added that I would never ever hurt any cows because they are special. I also added that I wouldn't shoot any Indians, which I thought was a nice little joke because there are Indians and Indians.

As I was moving through the bush I saw that Lisatoa was following me. Seeing him took me by surprise, stopped me thinking about *Bonanza*, and I wondered what he wanted. Maybe he wanted me to thank him for getting Alex to stop slapping me; that made sense, so I said, "Howdy there, much appreciated for you riding to my rescue back there. I owe you." As soon as I'd said those words, I knew how stupid they sounded. Guess I hadn't completely stopped thinking about *Bonanza*. I also hoped I didn't speak in an American accent with a tough-guy sneer on my lips, like I did when watching my shows and had to warn the good guys that something bad was about to happen. It's something I'm still pretty good at; I put it down to years of bathroom mirror practice. Sometimes I think I might watch too many cowboy shows. I will definitely cut back, in a couple of years; eighteen sounds like a good cut-off point. With Lisatoa still following me into the bush, I congratulated myself that at least I hadn't called him pardner. I even thought I must have gotten away with the cowboy stuff because Lisatoa didn't say anything, which was a bit of a relief. When I stopped and turned around again, he looked at me and said, "We will become friends."

I didn't know what to say when he said that. But I did know having a friend would be super-duper nice. Lisatoa just stood there, not really looking for any sort of answer. When I walked deeper into the bush, I knew he was following me and at first it felt like I was doing something that I didn't want to do. I could've stopped, I could have turned around and walked back through the rubbish and back to my place. But I didn't do that, I kept walking into the bush. Which I think must tell you something. Soon he was walking beside me, and though this was my bush, it was like we were both leading the way. At first, we came to the old settler's hut, grey timber walls still standing, corrugated roof collapsed and rusting. Out the back of the hut there's the remains of an orchard: gnarled lemon trees with bitter, thick-skinned fruit; a mulberry tree, its trunk split and rotting; an apple tree, fallen fruit scattered around. A little further I shared the secret of the hollow in the giant gum and showed Lisatoa three ring-tailed possums cuddled close and starring out wide-eyed and wary. I took him to the gorge, carved through honey sandstone by a small tributary that flows into the river that passes Lisatoa's house. I pointed out my caves, led him into one and showed him the paintings. Steered clear of the cluster of grass trees and the smooth rocks in between where the brown snakes like to sun themselves. Cupped our hands and slurped water from a small, clear stream, then wandered back until we arrived at the rubbish, which seemed to look a lot more out of place and ugly. Neither of us had spoken a word, except for Lisatoa's initial, "We will become friends." We continued to stand there a few moments longer, before Lisatoa turned and began to move away. He didn't say it loudly, but I still heard him: "I best mosey on back to my ranch now." I knew he wasn't being nasty to me, not making fun of me. Nice for a change. Maybe if I really was a cowboy I wouldn't just have my friendly horse, perhaps a pardner too.

When I got home that day I asked mum if I could have big plate of chips for dinner. She said, no.

Lisatoa lived in a big house right beside the river and I loved going there because it felt good in his house. In fact it was just good to be asked over to a friend's place. It was my second favourite house. There was always a lot of noise there: music playing, sisters arguing, the yapping of two Pomeranians, the strange accents of his parents' voices singing the songs of other countries. It might have been noisy in Lisatoa's house, but in my head I always felt comfortable and calm. The house was built on stilts to keep it safe when the river flooded. Lisatoa and I liked to sit on the top verandah and look out at the river through the branches of a camphorwood tree; we didn't talk, we just sat and watched the river. This was a really nice thing to do. Sometimes the river glistened diamonds in a morning sun, or turned golden in a sunset, sometimes the water was a happy spritely blue, other times a grumpy, moody brown. The river is a bit of a character. When the river moved really fast, you could see the swirling current and you'd know that it would be a bad time to fall in. Other days the river would be all relaxed and sleepy, just slowly meandering, different birds happy to float and drift along. Quite often Lisatoa would go and get his sketchbook and pencils. I liked watching him draw, how a blank white page could come to life. Sometimes he'd draw the curve of the river, trees lining its banks, a tethered dinghy. Other times a single leaf of the camphorwood, or a section of its bark. At first, he wouldn't show me his drawings, but now he's happy to do that. I show him my writing, so it's a fair trade.

Lisatoa's dad is a giant. He's originally from Samoa and he would tell outrageous stories about how he was kidnapped by pirates until he escaped and came ashore here. His name is Iosepha. Sometimes he would tell us how the leader of the pirates was his Scottish wife and how she quickly fell in love with her Samoan captive. I didn't think his pirate stories were anywhere as good as the high-seas adventures of Tobias and his mum that I told the class each Friday afternoon. Though I did borrow a couple of his ideas. Lisatoa's dad had a workshop at the back of the house. He made all sorts of things out of wood, ranging from simple salad bowls to intricate statues. People commissioned him to do these statues. The statues all had these strange and interesting details, drawn from Samoan stories of Gods and Goddesses, of peacemakers and warriors. I thought it a little spooky in the workshop to begin with, like I was being watched over by the wooden statues and that they were waiting to do something evil. But Lisatoa's dad let me help him out with some of his work and the perfumed smell and feel of the wood put me at ease. At first, I didn't want to help out, mainly because I didn't think I could, felt I would just mess things up. "I haven't got the hands to do woodwork," I told him. But Iosepha just laughed aloud, got some wood and put it in a clamp, telling me, "That will hold it, take the plane and the sandpaper, get to know the wood. Wood's not interested in what you have or don't have, just wants to be made beautiful and useful." I didn't know what to say back to him, so I just turned around and started on the wood. And I managed, and I liked it, though I did get a tired arm and sore hand that first time. Later, I thought of those statues as watching over us, wanting to take care of us.

The most beautiful statue was the biggest one, standing about five foot tall. It's not a statue that was for sale. It stood in the corner of the workshop on a large block of wood. It could see everything that went on in the workshop. The wood of the statue was a beautiful mix of colours which seem to change depending on the light. Initially I thought the colour of the statue might have seemed to be changing because of whatever mood I was in, like if I was happy it would seem to glow soft and warm, and if I was in a bad mood it would seem a little darker and duller. The hands of the statue were folded across its chest and one hand held a bunch of flowers that looked like hibiscus and frangipani, while the other grasped a club that had all these nasty spikes sticking out of it. Looking at the mouth of the statue it sometimes seemed to be smiling, while other times it looked more a snarl. The eyes were a bit like that too; sometimes they seemed all shiny as if they were laughing at something funny, while at other times they looked all serious and brooding, as if someone was about to be in a lot of trouble. It was as if there was someone inside the statue, or the statue was more than a statue. I suppose this all sounds a bit crazy about a statue. I mean, it's just a statue, right? I asked Lisatoa's dad if the statue had a name and he said, "Depends", which was either not much of an answer, or a stupid name.

In the back corner of Iosepha's workshop Lisatoa had a space where he did his painting and drawing, a large window giving his "art space" plenty of good light for him to work in. At first it looked like messy chaos to me, a place filled with dirty brushes, jars of murky water, flat pieces of ply smeared with paint, dozens of discarded tubes and little bottles, scrunched-up balls of paper and half-finished drawings. Now I think it looked interesting, a place where something special was getting made.

I've been coming into Iosepha's workshop for years now and I still love it. I might be all grown up and fifteen, but the workshop still gives me the same special feeling that it did that first time. The only difference now is that each time I'm there I go over to the big statue, pat him on the back and tell him thank you for whatever part it was that he played; it's the least he deserves.

Lisatoa's mum's name is Ethel. She is a small woman with fiery red hair who always had a different book in her hand, which was easy for her to do because every room in the house had lots of books lying about. It was a house full of books and it was lovely. Still is. I was always allowed to look at and read any of them that I wanted. At first I liked a lot of the poetry ones, which came as a nice surprise as if I'd discovered some hidden treasure that would last me forever. I didn't even have to understand the whole poem, sometimes it was just a few lines that jumped out at me looking all special and shiny-fresh. I still liked stories best, novels, but poetry was coming a close second. I didn't tell anyone that I liked poetry, because people can get nervous around intellectuals. But I remember thinking Gina would understand if I told her. In fact, that's what I'd decided to do should the perfect opportunity arise, tell her I liked poetry because of all its poetic qualities.

If Ethel wasn't reading she would be at her typewriter writing stories and articles to sell to different magazines. I think that would be an okay job, even though she said it didn't pay much money. Ethel is from Aberdeen in Scotland, and sometimes, especially if she spoke quickly, I found it a little hard to understand her accent, but I paid close attention and slowly got better at knowing what she was saying. In fact, now at fifteen I don't have any trouble understanding everything she says which is just as well because I wouldn't have liked to miss her telling me she was writing a children's book, a novel. She looked me straight in the eye and said, "I was wondering if, when I get a bit more of it down, I was wondering if you might have a wee look at it and tell me what you think?" It probably won't surprise you then that as soon as I'd finished writing about Lisatoa and his family the person I asked to read it for me was Lisatoa's mum. "Call me Ethel," she said. "Us writers must be first name friends."

Lisatoa is a mixture of his mum and dad. He is powerfully built, just like his dad. When we wrestled, which was something I probably shouldn't have done, he always won, easily. He even won when I cheated outrageously, or when he tied one hand behind his back, which never evened things up at all. He could throw and kick a ball for miles and lift stuff like big logs, a tea-chest full of books, furniture, and even Alex when that became necessary. I couldn't do any of that stuff, at least not like Lisatoa could. But that doesn't mean I didn't like playing ball with him and wrestling, just that I did it for reasons other than winning. Unlike his dad Lisatoa isn't tall, and I reckon he got that from his mother, along with that red tinge to his hair that makes him look like a wonderful mixture. I look mostly like my mum, except my skin is a little lighter.

Lisatoa has two sisters. Moana was ten, a year younger than Lisatoa. Linda was seven. All three of them got on really well. Sure, they had their arguments, but even that was like they're playing or acting.

When I was eleven Lisatoa was the best friend I ever had. I'm fifteen now and, thank Krishna, nothing has changed.

I think that should about do it for my introduction to Lisatoa and his family. Time to rest my HB friends. I spread them over the small desk in my bedroom, no straight, boring lines for my pencils. I fan them out, close my eyes and imagine that my pencils are a group of writers and artists lolling around on some grassy hillside after a day of making magic. They wear clothes like in Shakespeare's time and are holding quills and paint brushes while drinking lots of vino.

Gosh, I really am getting all creative and imaginative; if I finish, no, *when* I finish MY PROJECT I think I might give poetry a bash.

SPARTACUS AND OTHER HEROES

It wasn't pretty, but it was effective. There was a lot of thrashing going on, the water bubbling and turbulent all around him, but he got to wherever he was heading, and he got there fast. I'm not a swimmer, obviously, but even if I was Lisatoa would have beaten me so easily. At the council pool kids stopped responding to his "race you there" challenges. He was faster than anyone I knew, except the lifeguard at the pool, but he didn't count because he was somewhere in his twenties and had swum competitively for his state; I'd seen his awards in the cabinet in the poolhouse, proudly on display, but slowly fading a verdigris green. Everyone called our lifeguard Skull, because his head was shaved. His real name was Trevor, which was a much nicer name. People only called him Skull behind his back and I think that's wrong, not evil wrong, just not right. People shouldn't call other people names. It's not being clever or funny. It's certainly something I've never ever liked. Enough said about name calling, I don't like to dwell on the subject. Apart from our lifeguard, Trevor, no one could beat Lisatoa, and the longer the race the greater the distance he would win by, like at the District Swimming Carnival where schools came from all over to compete.

I looked forward to the swimming carnival, set out early, beach towel all soft and smelling good tucked under my arm, thongs slapping as I hurried along. It was the first swimming carnival I had ever attended; I'd managed to avoid all previous ones at other schools by being "sick". The day was perfect swimming carnival weather, early morning promising a hot day. The pool wasn't far from the school, so we were able to walk there. Miss started out trying to get us to march in two straight lines, but that was a bit of a failure. She also wanted us to sing The Grand Old Duke of York, and that was a lot of a failure. Kevin was the only one to start singing, but when he changed into the theme tune to

The Flintstones Miss told him, three times, that he could stop now. As we got close, everyone hurried through the turnstile, keen to get a piece of the fifteen-minute free swim before the carnival officially started. Kids piled into the pool, like those descriptions of lemmings madly racing over the side of some cliff. Don't know why no one drowned, got knocked unconscious, or had some broken bones. Must have been a nightmare for the lifeguard. The whole pool looked to be alive, so many coloured costumes thrashing and splashing, so much screaming and yelling. I didn't join in the free swims, but I didn't feel too bad about that; it was still nice to stand on the edge of the pool and to walk barefoot in the warm water that spilled over the edges. Even the chlorine smelt good. To this day, I still refuse to believe Stephan's theory that the water was always so warm because everyone peed in it. Mind you, I wouldn't get into the toddlers' pool.

Lisatoa was entered in six different races, which sounded exhausting to me. All the other competitors at the carnival had had swimming lessons, it was obvious. When they swam they were smooth and sleek in the water, dolphin-gliding along their lanes with their skin-tight speedos, goggles and swimming cap, shadowed by cheering parents dancing strange jigs along the side of the pool. Lisatoa didn't need goggles or swimming cap, because he never put his head under the water; even with his starting dive, more the floundering bellyflop, his head stayed above water. Others would be way ahead at the start, but it never mattered. Their smooth turns, compared to Lisatoa's awkward about face, didn't help them.

"It shouldn't be allowed, not swimming. He's like a washing machine," one parent whined, loud enough for other parents to hear, hoping they could become a chorus of complaint. This parent had run along the side of the pool in every race that his son was in. If Lisatoa wasn't in the race, his son would win. As he ran along the side of the pool, floppy sun hat bobbing up and down, he was continually yelling at his son, something I couldn't see much point in because if someone's head is under water most of the time they can't be hearing too much. But that didn't stop this parent yelling, getting louder and more excited with each lap, almost as if he thought he was swimming in the race and not his son. As well as yelling as he went along, this parent also had a huge movie camera attached to a strap around his neck, which he seemed to have glued to his right eye filming every move his son made. As he moved past us we could see the words WIN! WIN! written in zinc cream on each side of his hat.

At the end of the day, Lisatoa had won all six of his races, four of which the yelling parent's son had been in. Miss had gathered our class at the side of the pool. She did a roll call and started showing lost items that had been handed in, giving sandals, towels, water pistols, underwear and goggles back to kids who seemed surprised to find that they had lost something. Just down from us the yelling man was talking to his son, whose head hung down. It didn't look like a very happy way for someone to be finishing a swimming carnival. Just before Miss was to take our class back to school, she patted Lisatoa on the back and said, "Three hearty British cheers for the winner." She then held his right arm high, like he'd been the winner of a boxing match.

As Miss moved our class off, the yelling parent just stood there at the edge of the pool. He pushed back his sun hat and glared at Miss as if she was somebody he had hated for a long, long time. "Shouldn't be allowed," he said again. "Should be disqualified." He then looked Miss in the eye, Miss and the class stopping right beside him, and said, "Not that I expect some Pommy girlie to understand." This parent had a rude streak and a sore loser streak and a nasty streak.

The whole class went quiet, all other noises of the carnival seemed distant and fading. I'd never spoken up before, even for myself, but heard myself telling the parent, "Miss is not a "Pommy" or a "girlie". And you should stop whinging." Then I chucked in "Bozo," for good measure. I know it wasn't much of a response, but it still made me feel good. It felt good, not because it was some strong, cutting remark, but because for the first time it felt as if it could be the start of something, the beginning of doing or saying something when silence just isn't enough. "Mighty oaks from little acorns grow," Miss was often telling us; made a bit more sense to me then it did.

For a moment the parent just stood there, folding chair under one arm, small duffle bag in the other, large camera still around his neck. An ugly sneer started to spread across his face, like spilt black ink might grow and darken blotting paper. He took a step back and looked me up and down. "Don't look like you'd make much of a swimmer. Unless you count swimming in circles." Shaking his head, he grinned at me, then added, "No, my little suntanned friend, nothing sporty for you." The parent now seemed to be nothing but that ugly sneer, the blotting paper fully black. He tilted his head back and started to laugh loud and long. This parent also had a fully developed racist streak and a complete idiot streak.

There was a low grumbling from the class, a fidgety bubbling and bobbing movement like water starting to boil. Gina yelled out something loud and angry that must have been in Italian. The whole class was milling around the parent, like some disturbed nest of ants, kids scurrying in different directions, but always close to the parent. Someone swore. "Ouch, that's my foot," another cried. More swearing. "Jugofsaliva, Jugofsaliva," Stephan called out, while at the back of the class I glimpsed Alex pretending to shoot the parent with an invisible machine gun. Gina was still yelling in Italian when an arm shot out, the briefest flash, a lightning bolt, and pushed the parent backwards; he stumbled a little, dropped his chair and bag and began flailing his arms. As if in slow motion he fell back into the pool where his flailing arms continued their useless efforts. "Can't swim," he gurgled, "I can't swim." Later, I would think what a wonderful irony that was. No longer a disturbed nest of angry ants, the whole class fell silent and still, all eyes peering over the edge of the pool as if witnessing some fascinating curiosity. I can't be certain, but I think his son may have been one of the onlookers. At the other side of the pool I saw the lifeguard dive in and start towards the floundering parent. That lifeguard really could swim.

When the lifeguard got to the parent, he put one arm around him and said, "You can stand here, it's not deep." Half the class started to laugh, and once again I'm not sure, but it's possible his son joined in. Getting the parent out of the pool wasn't an easy task, the lifeguard had to try three times to heave him onto the side. His sun hat remained in the water, swirled around a few times then began to sink, the words written on the side slowly disappearing along with it.

Once out, water streaming down his sides, pooling at his feet, he spat out a mouthful of water. Stephan told him, "Lot of pee in that water." Kids laughed, but not the parent who put his hands on his hips and said, "Someone's gonna pay, tell you that, this camera cost a fortune, and someone's gonna pay." His right arm went out, finger jabbing as he pointed at different people. "You push me, did you? How about you, my washing machine swimmer, was it you? You there, you hiding at the back there, was it you? Someone's gonna pay, cost a fortune this camera, cost a fortune." He kept jabbing his finger at different members of the class. "You, was it you? Someone is gonna pay, that's a definite. Assault is what it was, it was assault. And destroying valuable property. So, who pushed me, who was it? Who was it?"

It was Gina who stepped forward. "I'm Spartacus," she said.

"What? What, what are you talking about?" the parent asked.

Lisatoa held both his arms high, "I'm Spartacus."

"Who's Spartacus? Can't be both of you," the parent said.

Someone else yelled, their voice strong and loud, "I'm Spartacus."

"I'm Spartacus," I said, "I'm Spartacus."

Two kids, somewhere at the back of our class, called out together, "I'm Spartacus."

There was then a ragged chorus of kids calling out, "I'm Spartacus. I'm Spartacus. I'm Spartacus."

Stephan was about the last person in my class to step forward. I thought I knew what he was about to say, but was wrong. Stephan puffed his chest out, beat it twice like Tarzan would, and said, "I'm Spartacus, I'm Spartacus." Later, I thought he did that because he knew this wasn't a joke, just not the time for one. Told you I'd like the Spartacus story even more.

In the end there wasn't anything the parent could do; unlike the Spartacus story he couldn't crucify all of us. "Maybe, you just slipped in the pool. See it all the time. Accident, you know," the lifeguard said, just as Miss was hurriedly telling the class to move off, "Quickly now. Chop, chop. Mustn't be late. Hurry now." I was one of the last people to follow Miss. I turned to face the parent, who still stood there dripping. "You even look like a bozo now," I told him.

In the end, I'm pretty certain that every person from our class had stepped up and said, "I'm Spartacus." Except for Miss, which was a bit odd because I'd seen that it was really Miss who was Spartacus. Clearly, Miss has a fully developed mischievous streak. Who'd have thought? I think my larrikin streak is a bit like Miss' mischievous streak, so no wonder I think she's the best teacher in the world.

When I got home that day, I had that warm tiredness that comes from spending a day in the sun. During dinner mum asked how the carnival had gone and I told her how Lisatoa had won all his races, but I didn't tell her much more.

In bed that night, slowly drifting off to sleep, I thought about the swimming carnival. I told myself how it had been a good day, beautiful weather, Lisatoa winning all his races, the lifesaver showing how he could really swim like a champion and how Spartacus had won the day. I thought about how that parent had slapped me down. But I also thought about how I'd gotten back up again. Acorn growing. Yeah, I had a lot of good things to remember about that day, but still there was a bit of me that fell asleep feeling a tiny bit sad.

THE RIVER GOD

Lisatoa did most of his swimming in the river that flowed past his house; he'd run along the jetty behind his house and dive right in. Sometimes I'd get in the water too, splashing and lolling around. Water could be fun without having to swim in it! I could keep my head above water, but it was always a bit of a struggle and the kicking of my legs to push me along was tiring. At first it made me feel awkward, thinking everyone watching would really notice me. But no one seemed to pay me any attention, I was just another kid fooling around in the water. In the end if anyone was noticing me, well, I didn't notice them noticing, I just got on with having fun. And having fun in the water was something that that parent from the swimming carnival, the one with the rude, sore loser, nasty, racist, complete idiot streak, had tried to take away from me. Bad luck, he failed! (Thank you Spartacus.) The other thing I used to enjoy on the river was floating in a large inner tube, sitting in it like it was some sort of water hammock, closing my eyes and letting the current carry me along; it felt soothing, like I was being taken care of by something invisible and more powerful than myself. "That's the River God," Lisatoa told me, "usually a friendly, calm god, but he can get angry at times." I couldn't imagine what an angry River God would look like. I'm sorry I ever found out.

One of those angry times was when it had been raining heavily for a week and the river had swollen and was surging and growling past, brown water churning around the pylons of the jetty like watery chocolate. The wooden steps at the end of the jetty that let you walk down to the water had been snatched away, leaving some ugly nails jutting out. Two canoes remained tied to one of the jetty's pylons, the rope holding them stretched and taut, the canoes looking as if they wanted to escape and run with the wild water. Branches, sometimes whole trees, were carried along. We saw a door, some paint tins, two chairs, someone's dinghy and two eskies. Then in the surging water, other side of the river, we saw some animal trying to keep its small head above water. Through the driving rain we could see it struggling, sometimes its head rising a little, only to go back under. Then we saw its head disappear and it seemed an age before it resurfaced. We thought it must be a wallaby. Standing on the jetty, both of us were willing it to stay afloat, sending waves of hope and energy. Then it got tangled up in the branches of one of the trees that had been washed along, a tree that was momentarily slowed by all the rubbish in front of it, a temporary logjam. Water was surging over the wallaby's head, but still it struggled, it would put up a fight to the end. I started to turn away, I didn't want to see the poor thing die, I knew what was going to happen, but I just didn't want to see it.

I then heard a shout from Lisatoa and turned in time to see him jump off the end of the jetty and into the river. I screamed at him; something terrible, something unthinkable, was going to happen and I screamed at him till it felt my throat was being torn apart, but still I kept screaming because I just couldn't stop. Lisatoa swam at an angle across the river; there was no way he could have beaten the current to swim straight across. Sometimes he seemed to be making progress, only to be pushed aside. But he never looked back, he would not give up. There were moments when it looked as though something being washed down the river would collide with him, hit him, knock him unconscious, but he always managed to avoid it. At that moment, I wanted to dive in to help him, and even if it were possible for me to do that I wondered if I would have had enough courage. It was a big, big question.

It seemed ages before Lisatoa got to the other side where the wallaby was still caught in the branches of the tree. When he got there, I felt my whole body slump in relief, letting out a gasp of air, some breath held too long. He had made it, and he could free the wallaby, push it ashore, and I could get his parents to drive down alongside the river, cross the bridge and pick him up. But that wasn't going to happen because my crazy friend had grabbed the wallaby with one arm around its neck, and like a rescuing life-guard he was starting to swim back across the river. I started waving my arm, windmilling like crazy, but he paid no attention. I began screaming at him again, louder than ever. I pictured my raw throat bleeding now, blood gushing down my throat.

Lisatoa was about two thirds of the way back when I felt the presence of people behind me. Turning around, I first saw Moana and Linda shivering and huddled together. Beside them stood Lisatoa's parents and I knew this would not be good. Lisatoa was still making progress, but it was hard work and I knew he was starting to lose strength, starting to weaken. I suddenly realised that my friend couldn't always be strong, couldn't always win the race, couldn't always save the day and I felt a little sad, like finding out about Santa Claus or that Superman wasn't real. But I also felt kind of good, like it brought us closer to a truth, to a reality that said we're both little humans, we're both real and we're both friends. You wouldn't think someone could be sad and happy at the same time, but it is possible. It was then that I got an answer to that big, big question. I knew then that if it were possible, I would jump into the river.

Lisatoa had only thirty or forty feet more to go when a large, uprooted tree, tumbling and twisting, came rushing towards him, broken branches looking ugly and sharp, ready to impale both Lisatoa and the wallaby. One of the branches narrowly missed, but others were soon following. With his free arm Lisatoa grabbed a branch and for a moment was dragged along. I heard him cry out and through the sheeting rain could see a large brown snake moving sleek and fast along the branch. As the snake raised its head ready to strike, Lisatoa cried out again and let go of the branch and pushed off. But the snake had been committed to its strike and launched towards Lisatoa, falling just a few inches from its target. Lisatoa and the wallaby disappeared beneath the water. The snake paused a moment before swimming back to the relative safety of the disappearing tree. Lisatoa's head broke the surface, coughing and spitting water. He cried out again, this one a scream of anger and frustration; he'd lost the wallaby, all that striving, all that risk and danger, all that hope, and the wallaby was lost. A short distance from Lisatoa two of the wallaby's back legs appeared, frantically scratching at air and water, trying to right itself, fighting for a breath, fighting for life. Lisatoa lunged towards it, arms flailing with fading strength. With a last effort he reached the wallaby and held its head above water.

I thought my heart must have stopped beating, my breathing was shallow and fast. I felt light-headed and told myself breathe, deep breath, breathe, deep breath. It was then that a very large hand came down on my shoulder; it felt as if that hand was steadying me, planting me in the here and now. My head cleared and breathing settled as Iosepha leaned into my ear and told me to, "Sing him back. Tie him with sound, sound from deep inside, and sing him back. Maybe you have it, just maybe. Trust." I had no idea what he was talking about. He then stood upright on the edge of the jetty and ripped his shirt off and threw it into the river. When he turned to face me I could see his entire chest was filled with the curves and swirls of strange paintings, bright yellows and oranges, dark blues, slashes of red; strange paintings that I had seen before.

Iosepha turned away from me, faced the river and began this loud humming sound, long and drawn out, only briefly punctuated by an intake of breath. He looked bigger, much bigger than I'd ever thought him to be, as if he'd suddenly grown. I didn't know what we were doing, what it meant, but I found myself joining in, eyes locked on Lisatoa and humming as loud as I could. My throat didn't feel so sore anymore and it was as if our humming, loud and resonant, was quietening the river's angry growling. While I kept up my humming I felt this strange need to stretch out both arms in front of me, as if trying to reach hold of something. I first put out my right arm, then slowly my left. It probably looked silly, but I just felt it was something I had to do. All the time Iosepha and I were doing this, I was aware that just behind us Lisatoa's mother was jumping up and down yelling all sorts of threats at Lisatoa, promising a thrashing, starvation and being locked up forever.

I like to think that we "sung him back, tied him with sound from deep inside", but it might have been Lisatoa's perseverance and strength, perhaps a brief shift in the River God's mood, or just luck. The first one is the nicest to think, a bit magical, but I'll take any of them, thank you very much.

When Lisatoa made it to the end of the jetty he grabbed hold of the nearest pylon. He was clearly exhausted, but still clung onto the rescued animal; he was not going to let it go. Not then, not ever. I saw then that it wasn't a wallaby he was holding, but some sort of dog. Iosepha leant over the side of the jetty, so far over that I thought he would fall into the river, and reached down his right arm towards Lisatoa and said, "Hand." Lisatoa reached out his free arm, the other still holding tight to the dog, and Iosepha grabbed hold of it and with one arm began lifting Lisatoa and the dog out of the river. It should not have been possible, but I was watching it happen. Maybe it was like those times when you hear about a person lifting a car off someone trapped beneath it. Slowly Lisatoa and the dog were being hauled up onto the jetty. The tendons on Iosepha's arms looked as if they could snap at any moment and his face appeared ready to explode. But he did it. And in that moment I thought I could be wrong, maybe Superman is real.

And then out of nowhere it just jumped into my mind. Though maybe not out of nowhere. Dads are strong I thought, because they just won't let go, want to pull you closer, and no matter how hard it is they find a way. Postcards.

Lisatoa's mum came rushing forward, telling him that he was going to get a lesson that he'd never forget. She then looked at me and said, "I'm going to give you a thrashing too. My feather duster is going to clean both of you up!" Lisatoa had told me how his mum could turn a feather duster into a stinging weapon of punishment, just by holding the feather section and using the cane handle to swipe and wack bare legs. "Better swordsman than Robin Hood," he said. But we didn't get the feather duster. Instead Lisatoa's mum called out, "Everyone together now, draw close, everyone draw close! All six of us cuddle into one. Now!" She held her arms out, drawing us all in as if she was some magnet and we had no choice but to come together. It felt warm and right as she held us tight and close, all the time kissing Lisatoa's head and telling him what an idiot he was, completely mad, what were you thinking, you're never getting out ever again, bloody inconsiderate.

When we separated, Lisatoa put down the small dog. It was like a small greyhound, a whippet we later found out. Even just out of the muddy river water I could see that it had a lovely fur of mottled grey. Its watery eyes were large and soft, eyes that made you want to wrap your arms around it and hold it close; eyes that seemed to be saying thank you. And I do think that she (it was a girl dog) was saying thank you, because I believe animals are a lot smarter than we'll ever understand. But the thing most outstanding about the dog, the thing about her you couldn't miss, was that she only had three legs, her front left leg was completely missing, which made it even more incredible that she had managed to survive in the river at all. Lisatoa bent down and picked up the dog, telling her, "You are special, you are a gift." I looked at the dog with its missing front left leg and I felt a little strange, there was something not quite clear to me, like a message that I should understand. Lisatoa, along with the dog, walked back towards the house, his mother's arm around him. I didn't think there was going to be any thrashing. Never had. I stayed on the jetty, standing there, wondering.

A few moments later Iosepha and I followed behind. I asked him, "What did you mean back there when you said, 'Maybe you have it'? Have what? And 'trust', trust what? What did that mean?" He didn't answer me, kept walking as if I'd said nothing. I tried again, "Our singing. 'Sing him back', you said. What's that about? This tying him with sound?"

Iosepha stopped and turned towards me. He then placed a hand on each side of my head, pressing hard enough to feel uncomfortable. "Hmm," he said, and in that brief moment I wondered if he was trying to push something into my head or searching for something already there. But I thought about it in a distant way, as if it were some interesting curiosity and not really my head at all, as if I was standing a short way off and watching me. "Hmm," he said again, "unexpectedly deep some rivers, unexpectedly deep. More than a maybe, more." He then took his hands away and walked off. The sides of my head felt warm.

That night I took out all the postcards, looked at some of the pictures and read the writing. I gathered them into one bundle and put them in order before putting them away. One step at a time.

Going to sleep that night I felt I should thank Krishna for saving Lisatoa. Since Ethel had been there, I thought I should also thank Jesus. Then out of respect for the power of rivers I added Goddess Ganga. I thanked the River God, even though I wasn't too certain whether he'd caused the problem or if he'd rescued Lisatoa and given him a dog by way of compensation. This thanking the gods was getting a little out of hand; I imagined a line of different gods queued up so that they too could be thanked, and I didn't want to leave any of them out in case they got angry and upset. I blamed mum, because it's her books that have dozens and dozens of Hindu gods in them. And the books have these pictures in them that make it impossible not to keep looking. But thankfully there's also a goddess of sleep and she came to my rescue.

Now that I'm a mature fifteen I don't splash and frolic in the river so much. I prefer to relax in the back seat of one of the canoes Lisatoa and his family have. With Lisatoa paddling away we get to see a whole lot more of the river. I like to lean back and imagine we're explorers working our way up the Amazon, with thick jungle, lost civilisations and buried treasure around each bend. Or better still I'm in a gondolier in Venice, a famous writer researching his next worldwide super best seller. Back seat of a canoe is very good for my imaginative and writerly streak. It's just a pity that Lisatoa gets tired after a couple of hours and turns our canoe around. When I complain (politely), he tells me I was asleep anyway: he's clearly unable, despite our years together, to discern sleep from being in the thrall of the muse.

A LOOKER AND MORE

Lisatoa came into my life when I was eleven, saved me (though not like the dog from the river) and will probably go on saving me even though I'm fifteen. I didn't know that there would come a time when I could return the favour. I think it would be nice if everyone had someone who saves them. My mum has been saving me for a lot longer than Lisatoa, though in different ways. Just being there is a powerful way of saving someone. Thinking about my mum is sometimes a bit of a trap because it can lead to thinking about my dad. But okay, let me wander towards that trap and tell you about mum.

My mum is as strong as Iosepha, and though she doesn't have many big muscles she has been strong enough to hold things together. She has a strong streak, a genius streak, a wise streak and a loving streak. That's quite a few streaks and they work perfectly well together, mainly for me. She's been there all fifteen years of my life, right there in front of my eyes, though I might have been a bit blind a lot of that time. I started to see more clearly around the time mum had slapped Idiot Sir.

My mum's favourite room in the house was the kitchen and it's where you'd usually find her. "The kitchen is the heart and the belly of a home," she'd say. And in the heart and belly of our home my mum cooked me the best food in the world. It was unlike anything else you'd find around here, maybe even the whole country. Of an evening we'd sit at our little wooden table and eat our dinner, looking out the window at the people heading home from work. We thought they could smell our delicious food and it made their mouths water, even if they were in their car. At breakfast we'd sit at the same small table but looking out the window it was a different world we saw. I liked the clear sunny mornings when overnight rain made everything look brand new. Bower birds swooped down to the water of the birdbath, all muscular and frantic in their bathing, water spraying like a mini sprinkler. Later, the king parrots arrived, first taking their morning drink before quietly feasting on the seeds of Chinese elm or white cedar berries. Sometimes they'd hang upside down on some of the branches, show-off acrobats dressed in gaudy colours. "No," mum said, "not gaudy. Resplendent is much better; resplendent in their plumage." Then she giggled and said, "Bit much, perhaps." I didn't think it a bit much. I really liked that word, resplendent, it seemed to stick in my mind, and I wondered if there would be special times when I would get to use it. Whenever I said that word out aloud to myself, I thought it sounded rich and sparkly, magnificent and glorious even, just like the meaning of the word. On those clear sunny mornings with sun slanting across our kitchen floor even the small gathering dust balls or swirling motes looked good.

Mum cooked other stuff too, apart from what was for us, but that was for selling to Keane's Grocery and The Fruit Shop owned by Mr Vincenti. For those places mum cooked vegetable pies, cakes, fancy biscuits and any special orders they made. We didn't eat that sort of stuff, except sometimes. The vegetable pies didn't sell very well, unless some of the hippies made their trip into town. Mr Keane and Mr Vincenti kept asking mum to do meat pies and sausage rolls ("You'd make a few quid out of those, I can tell you."), but we didn't eat or cook any sort of meat. When I was in first class, ages and ages ago now, I mentioned this in my "Welcome to the Class" speech. It did not get a welcoming reaction from the class and especially the teacher, who said, "What absolute rubbish!" For years I never mentioned it again until I told Miss ("Bully for you Ray, bully for you.') and Lisatoa ("Big deal!"). Now, I don't care who knows or what they think. Mum says I don't have to not eat meat, I can make up my own mind, but for the moment I'm happy to eat just like mum. It's possible I'll change my mind one day, but I don't think so, because I can't think of anything better to eat than some of mum's samosas, naans and daal. Selling those cakes and biscuits was how mum "made ends meet." The other thing that helped mum "make ends meet" was the monthly allowance her parents made for her way back before I was born.

When we first got here the manager at Keane's Grocery tried to underpay mum. I guess he thought she'd be an easy target. He got that wrong. My mum has got a university degree from Oxford, so she is "educated and worldly", which she says is a good thing because it helps you get over the problems in life. Most times.

If the kitchen was the heart and belly of our home, then our loungeroom was the brain. It was a room filled with books, hundreds of books, most of which belonged to mum. Mum took boxes and boxes of her books with her when we moved here from Sydney. She packed them very quickly and that's why we still had some from Newtown Public Library. I had some books, but my collection was just starting out. There were no big lounges in our loungeroom, but there were two very comfortable chairs and we did a lot of lounging in them. Each chair had a tall and, I reckoned, expensive reading lamp beside it. Mine was made of wood, deep red in colour with carved monkeys climbing up it, forever trying to reach the carved palm leaves just below the light and its shade. Mum's lamp wasn't nearly good as mine, but her chair made up for it with its velvet material of swirling paisley. I often wanted to tell her that her chair was quite resplendent, but never did because if you use a word too many times it can lose its specialness, lose its shine. I still think that about words, because writers have to judge the right amount to use, just like mum does with chillies. I like words, getting better and better at using them now that I'm fifteen, though I don't know all that many good ones, but still, I like them. I think my use of words will probably be perfect when I'm eighteen, or nineteen at the latest. I also think MY PROJECT is helping me improve my use of words, which I think is great, grand and grandiloquent. (That last sentence has a tiny bit of a joke in it. I just chucked it in for amusement because you'd think the last word was a mixture of grand and eloquent. If you don't get the joke you shouldn't worry, it's not as if everyone *must* laugh at intellectual stuff.) Miss once told me "practice makes perfect", but I don't think that's completely true, because there're a lot of things I could practise at and I bet I'd never get perfect. Miss should have said "practice makes better".

This next bit about my mum isn't something I made up. It's what lots of people have said. People have said my mum is beautiful. Mum would walk into a shop and the man would say, "What can I help you with gorgeous?" When mum wasn't around, different men would tell me, "Gawd, your mum's a looker." One man, a shop assistant back in Sydney, leant over and whispered to me, "She's a real corker, streets ahead of that Twiggy. Not my type of course, no way. Just saying." I was glad when we left that shop. None of this sort of stuff was what mum liked to hear. Opposite in fact. She once told a bus conductor, who said she had "lovely eyes and lips," to "keep his adolescent behaviour in check and to get on with the task for which he is employed". He was lucky he didn't get the Idiot Sir slap.

I said how the food mum and I ate was different to anything else around. So were the clothes she wore. Her clothes were just so colourful; rich oranges and reds, bright yellows and deep purples like the stain of mulberries. I have never known her to wear anything else. "They tie me to my past, whilst letting me float free." There were times when I just had to tell her she looked resplendent; sometimes, I just had to use that word. The only occasion I'd seen clothes as colourful were the times the hippies came into town from their commune, wearing shirts of swirling colours, bright green pants or tie-dyed dresses. I remember the first time I saw them, pouring out of their van like a kaleidoscope of energy and colour. If smiles can have a colour theirs were sunny and bright. We were just outside Keane's Grocery when they arrived in their painted van. They were going into the shop, but three of them spent a long time talking to mum. I couldn't hear what they were talking about, but the hippies seemed to be doing a lot of laughing and nodding of heads. Other people passing by gave them strange looks, sneers and grunts that were not friendly. I later asked mum what they had talked about and all she said was, "Philosophy, philosophy. I think they might call their commune an ashram."

My mum is nearly always happy and in a good mood. "Smiling costs nothing," she says, which isn't very Oxford-like, because lots of things cost nothing (like snarls, sneers, frowns, slaps and stupid questions, for example) and that doesn't make them good. I think Oxford let her down there. The most times I have seen mum sad or upset were to do with my dad. So, good riddance to him, I used to think. One other time was when I came home with my ten out of ten story about Tobias, but why that made her sad I have no idea. Mum was seated at the kitchen table, cup of black tea in front of her. I took a seat beside her and told her about my story. Straight away she said, "On your feet young man. The story, we will have your story or there'll be no supper." She smiled and leant back in her chair. I pretended I didn't want to read my "silly little story", even though I hadn't left it at school like I usually did with any other work. This time I read the story the way mum used to read to me, trying to give it a bit of drama; I really got into that reading, perhaps overdoing it a little. When I looked up, mum's eyes looked as if she might start crying. I asked her what the matter was, and she said, "Nothing, Ray, nothing. Except we should have had this reading in our loungeroom, that would have been the right place. That's all."

THE POSSUM INCIDENT AND THREATENING GODS

My mum says that difficult times can sometimes bring people to-gether, that sharing a rough and tough experience can create a bond. She then gives me a long list of examples where people "forged unbreakable allegiances and life-sustaining bonds". She told me about people during the blitz in London, prisoners of war in Changi, polar explorers, train crash survivors and soldiers in the trenches in World War 1. Mum did a lot of history at Oxford, so I knew she had lots more examples. I also know that history has a lot of examples where people are really horrible and selfish to each other during stressful times; I know this even though I have not been to Oxford. If I'd wanted to argue this with mum, I would have brought up the example of my dad leaving, but I didn't do that. Besides, I know she has a point and that what she says is true. Just not always true. I think of the time Lisatoa res-cued the whippet; it was true then. And the possum incident.

It wasn't very far into the bush where the three possums lived. They used to be my possums, but with Lisatoa sharing things just seemed natural and exactly what I wanted to do. I feel quite good when I share. Yet in the end sharing the possums wasn't such a good idea; some things should just be left alone, because that's best how they do what they're supposed to do.

Early evening was the time Lisatoa and I would visit our pos-sums. I'd go into the kitchen, open the bottom drawer and take out the little torch, grab us an apple each. The bush is different in the early dark of evening; the sharp light of day drains away and loud noises slowly fade. It's as if the bright sun and noise of day have gotten tired and need to settle down and rest. It's the time when little things get noticed: the crunching of feet on fallen leaves, a sharp crack of a snapping twig, the murmur and rustle of night life starting up, the slow beating wings of birds heading home, scuttling lizards in the undergrowth, the rattle of the evening's first crickets. And the breathing of someone walking beside you. It's a crowded silence.

I've tried to set the scene of early evening because Miss says it's important for readers to get a sense of time and place, even if it seems a bit boring to me. I told Miss I'd already done that when I described the day we moved into our home, as well as when I first showed Lisatoa the bush, and that should be enough scene setting for even the most demanding reader. Miss did not agree, so I double checked with Ethel who agreed with Miss. So, who am I to argue? Still, I'd rather describe what's happening rather than setting the scene. I wonder if that means I will become an action or adventure writer. I hear they make mountains of money, which I would also share. With certain people.

When Lisatoa and I would get to where the possums lived they'd usually still be in their nest, sometimes deep asleep and sometimes eyes just opening and slowly squirming in to wakefulness. Then other times, not too often, they'd be out of their nest and on one of the lower branches of the tree. If I shone my torch on them their eyes would glisten and look all shocked and even scared. I never stopped thinking how small and beautiful they looked and only when Lisatoa said to let them have their dark did I turn the torch off. Before going, I'd bite off some of my apple and rest the pieces on a nearby branch. After we'd been doing this for a while we were able to get really close to the possums and could place the apple right beside them. We knew that you probably shouldn't feed wildlife, but those possums seemed to like their bits of apple, and maybe they were starting to like us too. Sometimes, when we were leaving, I'd shine the torch on them one more time, just to be sure they really were that beautiful.

When we came back from visiting the possums, Lisatoa would often stay for dinner. I remember the first time he stayed for dinner. I was a bit nervous about our food. When we came into the kitchen it was filled with the smells of what mum had been cooking. I could see the stack of cheese naans, the chickpea curry and Bombay potatoes. It was my favourite meal, though I've got lots of favourite meals, like the Rajasthani onion and potato curry I'm trying to perfect. I worried what Lisatoa would think, maybe he wouldn't think it was proper food.

When Lisatoa came into the kitchen he started sniffing the air and looking around. When he let out a loud, "Whoa," I felt even more nervous, a sick feeling in my stomach. A couple of years ago, when we were still living in Sydney, I thought I had a new friend. His name was Barry and he had a broken leg from playing rugby league so had to spend lunchtimes in the library until his leg got better. Barry was really popular and his friends would pile into the library, but they were loud and noisy, even tried playing "footy" with one of the dictionaries, so they got thrown out. So, Barry spent a bit of time talking to me. I tried to teach him chess: "That what you guys play? Boring." I thought we were getting on a bit, kind of. And maybe that would be good for me, I thought, could be nice to have a friend. After school one day, Barry came back to my place. I helped him with his crutches up the step into our kitchen where mum was preparing dinner. Barry tilted his head back and let out a loud, "Whoa." He was quiet a moment, then looked at me and said, "Pong! It's just like they said." I was happy that Barry's leg got better and that he could play "footy" again.

What Barry said and did that time isn't what I remember most, it's not what makes me cringe when I think back on it. What I remember most is how I reacted: I just stood there, stupid grin on my face, my head nodding idiotically up and down as if I was in total agreement with him. I won't do that ever again. Not sure what I'd do, but it wouldn't be that.

So, when Lisatoa walked into our kitchen and let out a really loud "Whoa" I couldn't help feeling a little sick and nervous. "This smells fantastic, it's like a feast." He then just stood there in the middle of our kitchen, wide grin on his face and I felt like giving him a big thank you hug. I remembered how he ate more cheese naans than mum and I put together; they just disappeared one after the other. I liked sharing that dinner with Lisatoa, but I wouldn't have minded an extra cheese naan or two.

Then there came the time when we went to visit the possums and it didn't turn out so good. It had been a day of heavy rain and a thin white fog of humidity hung in the air as we moved into the bush. The ground was sodden in places and sometimes my thongs squelched and became stuck in the mud. I decided to walk barefoot and the ooze of mud between my toes and the soft mat of fallen leaves felt good. In mum's photos from India lots of the people are barefoot, so that's probably a good part of why I liked it.

When we got to the tree where the possums lived we only found one possum and he stayed deep inside the nest and couldn't be tempted by the apple. We looked for the other two, but saw nothing; they were always together, so this was unusual. We hoped the other two were off somewhere getting food or whatever. There was nothing we could do, which is what adults always tell you in order to comfort you when something has gone wrong. You'd think that adults, having been around for ages and ages, might have come up with something a bit better than "nothing you could do".

The next morning there was a cluster of students in the corner of the playground, a lot of chattering and high-pitched squealing. I was about to go and see what was happening when the bell rang and the group began to break up, so I moved off to class. It was during roll call that Alex came into class. Straight away I knew what was happening. I'm not even sure I'd actually seen anything before I knew, I just knew. Alex was carrying one of those cat cages, the sort you put your cat in when you're moving house or taking the cat to the vet. Only this time huddled in the back of the cage were two ring-tailed possums, our possums. I'd have recognised those little guys anywhere. I was out of my seat when I heard Alex saying, "Look Miss, I saved these from the jungle, the terrible jungle, the bad jungle." I scrambled around desks, knocking them aside, banged my right thigh on the sharp edge of Miss' desk, really hurting it, but I didn't stop, I was going to get those possums off Alex and then I was going to grab Alex and... but I never got that far. I could hear Miss' raised voice, something about obeying rules, unruly behaviour and to leave it up to her. No chance. Alex then let out a loud yowling sound, turned and ran out of the classroom, banging the cage hard against the doorway as he left. Miss continued her yelling for order and quiet, and I heard my name loud and clear and my being told to stop. But there are those times when you shouldn't stop. My larrikin streak was in charge.

Alex was making an awkward run across the playground, the cage waving madly from side to side. I wanted to stop chasing him, hoping he'd stop too, because I didn't want the possums being thrown around. But I knew Alex wouldn't stop, Alex always did what he wanted to do, and Alex always got away with it. And that's just not right, so I started chasing after him. I was chasing him to get our possums back, but I was also chasing him for other reasons: I was after him for slapping me in front of the whole school; I was after him for emptying Gina's school bag, and laughing at the small stuffed cat she had in there; I was after him for starting the fire in the boy's toilet, using all the toilet paper to get it going; I ran after him for having hot chips every single day. But most of all I was chasing Alex because back in Sydney there had been two sad budgies in a small cage in Idiot Sir's office. And I had not saved them.

So, I had plenty of reasons to be chasing after Alex, but my right thigh really hurt, and I was limping, but I still thought I could catch him, the sore and limping leg would go away and I would catch him. But there are times when no matter how hard you want to do something, it doesn't mean you can. One time I wanted to have a lend of this kid's billycart and ride it down this steep hill. He told me I wouldn't be able to use the rope to steer it, but I wanted to do it. Of course, in the end I couldn't steer it. I lost a lot of skin off my right hand and both knees. So, wanting to do something doesn't make you able to do it. But I kept going anyway, screaming in my mind for Kartikeya to help me, to make Alex trip over, maybe leave the cage behind, but Kartikeya must have been busy crushing evil somewhere else, so the distance between us grew. I swore at Alex, the worst words I knew, hoping the anger wrapped inside them would bring him down.

Suddenly, I felt that I was going to burst into tears, I wanted to stop running and to start screaming and crying as loud as I could. I wasn't being a very successful larrikin. It was then that I saw Lisatoa powering past me. It's another one of those things that I'll never forget. Like I said earlier, Lisatoa isn't tall like his dad, but he is powerfully built and when he went past me I thought of a steam train, all low and steely muscle, a powerful locomotive that just wasn't going to quit until it got where it needed.

When Lisatoa caught up to Alex, he grabbed him by the back of the shirt which ripped right down the front. I wasn't close enough to actually see it, but I like to think there was a lovely ripping sound with bottoms flying everywhere. Perhaps a startled cry of fear from Alex too. When I caught up to them, the first thing I did was to check on the possums; they looked shaken and scared, but otherwise okay. I put my right hand down to the sore spot on my thigh, there was a tear in my shorts and my hand came away with some blood on it. But I couldn't give it too much more thought because all my attention was drawn to what Lisatoa was doing. He seemed to have blown himself up to be as big as possible with this fearsome look on his face. He was snarling at Alex, telling him that if he ever went near the possums again, if he even went into the bush where they came from, then he would feed Alex piece by piece "to the hungry sharks and slimy eels that live with the River God and the curse of Tagaloa would be on him forever." Alex just stood there, a shocked look on his face.

Later I told Lisatoa he'd sounded scary and convincing and that I thought he had a pretty good imagination being able to come up with all that in the heat of the moment. He told me that he didn't make it up and that there are great gods like Tagaloa, there is a River God, all of which I thought was interesting, if a little confusing, because Lisatoa's family go to a small Presbyterian church every Sunday. When he was telling me that there really were gods like Tagaloa, I started shaking my head and laughing like I knew he was pulling my leg, but Lisatoa didn't join in. "You shouldn't laugh," he told me. "You've already met the River God. And he listened to you. So, no laughing." Which made sense when I thought about it later, because it also explained why Kartikeya didn't help me; Kartikeya knew some other god would be involved. I was glad there had been a reason for Kartikeya not rushing to my assistance; I'd spent several hours going through some of mum's books and memorising the gods I thought might come in handy. Good to know I hadn't wasted my time. I then started to wonder how the gods decided who's doing what, who's covering what problem, but decided to let that one go for the time being.

Whatever shock Alex had felt from Lisatoa's threatening words didn't last long. Alex spat at Lisatoa and lunged to grab him by the throat, but Lisatoa brushed his arms aside, charged forward like a tackle in rugby league to take hold of Alex around his middle. Lisatoa then put Alex onto his shoulders and despite Alex's kicking and screaming started to turn around and around. Finally, the spinning stopped and for the briefest of moments Lisatoa lifted Alex above his head like the strongman from the circus. It was very impressive, a little worrying about what might come next, but very impressive. Lisatoa didn't need any help from Tagaloa and the others.

When Lisatoa put Alex back down, Alex continued swearing, but there was no more spitting and when he turned around to leave there was a little wobble in his walk, like the drinkers leaving the Forest Arms walking to their cars.

We carried the two possums back into the bush, holding their cage between us. We didn't speak, but I did think about mum's "forged unbreakable allegiances and life-sustaining bonds". I knew Lisatoa and I already had that, but a little reinforcement from time to time couldn't hurt.

The possums took a while to leave the cage. We figured that Alex must have followed us one time and found our possums, possums that had become used to people and easy to lure into a cage. We only occasionally checked on them after that and we didn't give them apple or anything to eat. Still wished that their nest was higher up and that their tree was further in the bush. I think I will always remember how they looked when I shone the little torch on them. Encyclopedia Britannica says that they are lucky to survive to three years old. Bit of a sad deal, eh?

THE RICOCHET OF CIGARETTE BULLETS

Soon after the "possum incident" Alex MacGregor got sent to a special school and everyone knew that "special" in that sense wasn't like, "Your birthday is your special day" or "I've got a special surprise for you." Alex just kept getting into trouble and each time the trouble got more and more serious.

There was the time when Miss got each member of the class to "bring in their favourite leaf and to vividly and poetically describe the leaf and the tree it came from." I wondered if I was the only person who didn't have a favourite leaf. It was the beginning of autumn, though things don't change so dramatically around here just because the calendar flips over into March. It all sounded a bit boring, but not to Miss who showed us different pictures of English forests with these bright, colourful leaves. She then read us a poem called "To Autumn" by a writer called John Keats. I don't think anyone in the class understood the poem, no one was listening. I, however, paid attention as carefully as I could, tilted my head and put the perfect intellectual look on my face. This was because I was becoming quite expert in my knowledge of poets and poetry, having looked at tons of Ethel's books in Lisatoa's house. Plus, I thought I might be able to pick up some tricks of the trade, see how these poets do their thing. I didn't pick up any tricks, and I didn't fully understand the poem, but I sure liked the way some of the lines sounded. I could even picture some of the things Mr Keats wrote about. Miss said Mr Keats wrote that poem when he was twenty-four and that he died when he was twenty-five, which I think is very impressive, but also very sad.

Thursday morning was the time for us to bring in our leaves. Stephan came in with the leaf of a banana tree which was as tall and nearly as wide as he was. "This is a banana leaf. It is green. Bananas grow out of the end of the leaf." He wasn't particularly vivid or poetical. Or accurate. Kevin brought in a large gum leaf, telling Miss that the main feature of the leaf "wasn't its khaki colouring or its eucalyptus stink, but its musical notes". He then tried to get some musical notes out of his gum leaf, but only made some sounds that nobody much appreciated, apart from Stephan.

Gina came in with the leaf of a London Plane. I knew straight away that she just wanted to talk about a leaf that had London as part of its name, which I thought was a slightly underhand way to get extra points from Miss. However, I had to admit that she did have an awfully good leaf, large with bright red and orange colours. When I tried to get a London Plane leaf, I could only find ones that were still green or a dull, dirty yellow. As Gina passed my desk, heading to the front of the class to give her talk, she smiled at me and winked. She winked at me quite a lot, so it was just as well that I liked it. Bit funny, I thought, how someone moving an eyelid can make you feel okay. "The majestic leaves of London Planes," Gina said, "are somewhat similar in shape to Canada's maple. But I think the London Plane is the sweeter tree, even though it doesn't produce any syrup." Gina paused a moment to see if anyone was going to find her comments amusing. No one did, except Miss and she didn't count. And maybe Stephan giggled a tiny bit, but that didn't count either because I knew he was putting it on. "They are the famous trees of London where they grace the parks and streets of London. Their summer foliage provides London with much needed shade for busy Londoners, while their autumnal changes provide a riot of colour. The London Plane is also..."

Gina was sure getting her quota of "Londons" in when she had to stop mid-sentence. Alex had come into the classroom carrying a small tree, dirt still clinging to its roots. Everyone in the class knew that tree. Maybe not its name, maybe not where it originally came from or how long it could live, maybe nothing about its leaves, but everyone knew that tree; the complete silence said so. Alex started to shake the tree, bits of dirt flying everywhere. He stuck his head into the middle of the tree and started shrieking, "I'm in the jungle bang bang you're dead, cigarette bullets. Cigarette bullets kill, they kill. I'm in the jungle bang bang you're dead. Bang bang I'm dead. He's dead. I'm dead." He then started breaking off some of the smaller branches and throwing them around the room. "Gotta clear the jungle," he said, "Gotta clear..."

It was then that Miss arrived beside Alex, reached out her arm and took hold of the tree's small trunk. She didn't try to pull it out of his hands, didn't yell and scream at him, just quietly said, "Please Alex." Alex let Miss have the tree, his arms falling by his side. Miss then led Alex silently and wordlessly out of the room.

For a while the class stayed silent and still, frozen in the drama of what just happened. But it didn't last long. People began laughing, someone screamed, some books were knocked off the shelf, two boys were wrestling and chairs were toppled, balls of paper flew across the room. Someone starting chanting, "Mad and bad, mad and bad, he's mad and bad." Others joined in. The bell for morning playlunch rang, all chanting and movement stopped, then the class surged towards the door like water when the sink plug's pulled. In the middle of all that movement, I saw Gina jump onto Miss' desk, cup her hands around her mouth and yell, "Don't any of you dare! Don't anyone leave this room. That means you. Stand still!" And the class did what she said. Don't know how she did it, but no one moved. I looked at Gina standing there; she had very nice legs that would be good for climbing, running fast or playing soccer. I thought her school dress seemed a little too short, something Miss should do something about. Gina had strong, bulging calf muscles and her skin was a smooth and shiny light brown. I'd never noticed anyone's legs before, except mine when I get scabs on my knees.

I stopped thinking about Gina's legs when she yelled, "We're going to fix our mess before anyone leaves." She had a very loud voice, and that meant she had excellent lungs; Gina was sure building a list of good points. Still standing on the desk, Gina spotted someone inching their way out: "That means you. Take another step out that door and I'll jump down and bash you up, rip your hair out." Wasn't sure if that should be added to the list of good points. "And... and... Stephan will help me." Stephan was standing right beside me and looked a little shocked at first, then said, "I'm from Jugof... no, no, I'm Spartacus, I'm Spartacus." Maybe it was Gina who stopped the person leaving, maybe Stephan, maybe even Spartacus. Either way, the person stopped.

"We're going to tidy up this mess, fix up Miss' room. Yes, we are. Now, I want..." Someone said, "Shut up, not me." Another person said, "You do it, big mouth." Just then a ball of paper was thrown at Gina, some people giggled, and again there was a movement towards the door. The person beside Stephan mumbled, "Wog," but both Stephan and I heard it loud and clear, maybe because we had special hearing for that sort of stuff. The class continued to surge out, but all movement froze when everyone heard the sound of a face being slapped, a loud slap. "That's for you," Stephan said. "Now do what Gina says." The boy who'd been standing beside Stephan and me, the mumbler, stood there holding his left cheek.

"Now, we need to pick up those books, bin those papers and straighten desks and chairs." When no one moved she added, "Come on, won't take us a second." It was Stephan who was first; he started picking up the books and neatly stacking them back in place. Lisatoa was picking up papers and taking them to the bin and I began straightening some chairs, but by then most people were doing something to get the mess cleaned up.

It was Stephan who Gina had called on to help her bash someone up. It was Stephan who slapped the person who called Gina a name. Stephan was the first person to start tidying up the room. I wished it had been me that Gina had called on to help her bash someone up, though I knew that wouldn't have been the smartest choice. But still. And I knew it was wrong to slap someone, except for Idiot Sir who thoroughly deserved it. Yet I truly wished it had been me who'd done it. And I wasn't even the second person to start tidying up the classroom.

As we moved outside, I passed Gina's desk and could see that she had painted her leaf those bright red and orange colours. It might have been cheating just a bit, but I kind of admired it and wondered if Miss would have noticed, and even if she had would she have said anything.

Outside, I told Gina, "That was a lovely leaf. Bet Lisatoa couldn't have painted a better one." I thought I was mixing being clever and cheeky, but what I was really doing was trying to make up some lost ground, lessen a gap that had suddenly appeared.

"I suppose you had something better?" Gina asked. I told her how I'd brought in a cluster of berries from the white cedar tree in my backyard and that I was going to talk about how the birds can eat them, and how this helps spread the seeds around the country, and how the berries might look like little grapes but are poisonous to people. I said I had a berry to give to each person in the class for them to analyse. Gina just looked at me, grinned and said, "It's supposed to be about leaves, you knucklehead. Leaves!"

"Well, leaves just aren't my specialty. I should tell you that it's poetry that I like. Poetry and all its poetic qualities." Gina had nothing to say to that, so I was hopeful I'd won back a little ground.

Just before the end of playlunch, Gina, Lisatoa and I went over to the Memorial Garden. Stephan came too, though I don't think any of us asked him to; I know I most certainly did not! At the garden, Miss was crouched down, firming the soil around the re-planted English oak, while Alex was heading towards her carrying a bucket of water.

Apart from seeing Alex in the Memorial Garden, I had had a miserable day.

Then there was the time that Alex did something even more outrageous, a bit of a pencil catastrophe. Friday afternoon, and we'd just begun "Create a Story Time" when he started wandering past my desk. I reminded him that he wasn't allowed to leave his desk without permission, but he just looked at me. He then reached out and picked up my "Create a Story Time" 2B pencil, stuck it in his right ear, twirled it around and then put it back on my desk. Thankfully, I had two spare pencils, and used them from then on. I made sure that the pencil Alex had polluted stayed away from my other ones; it became the one I loaned out when someone asked. After school I told Lisatoa what Alex had done, but he couldn't have been listening too carefully because he didn't sound at all outraged about it. Gina must have overheard me though, because as she was leaving she said, "Stuck it in his ear? Oh well, could have been a whole lot worse." Which didn't bear much thinking about.

I sometimes wonder if the trauma of the pencil catastrophe worked on my subconscious and explains my devotion to writing MY PROJECT with HB pencils. But the subconscious is the dark, mysterious, and unknown region of our heads, so I don't suppose we'll ever know.

Eventually the trouble Alex created became dangerous. It was the lighting of fires that did it. We even found some different places in the bush where fires had been started, but luckily the bush was usually too wet to burn. But he did burn down the disused toilets in the corner of the playground. He came into class late after lunchtime and he wasn't long seated before we could see the lazy drift of smoke rising from the toilets. Half the class rushed to the window to see what was going on. Alex got a prime view by standing on his desk. Soon there were flames and the sound of fibro walls cracking and exploding. Everyone knew it was Alex and that look of crazy delight on his face confirmed it.

So, it was the special school for Alex after that. Miss told the class one Monday morning. Some kids cheered, but there was no "three hearty British cheers" coming from Miss. "Still, bit of a pity, sad really," she said. I don't know why, but a part of me agreed. It all felt a bit strange. Usually, if you don't like someone, that's it, you one hundred per cent don't like them. It's clear cut, end of story. I had a zillion reasons to dislike Alex, but yet ... Gosh, I thought, it used to be so much easier before, things were either completely black or completely white. And it's only gotten worse now that I'm fifteen!

BIRTHDAY PARTY

I had never liked going to parties. Not that I'd been asked to that many, except when kids" parents forced them to ask me. And that is not the sort of invitation anyone would want. I would not have gone to any of those parties, but mum gave me no choice: "Be good for you, get out and about, make some friends." For a great mum, she sure got that wrong. I would have pretended to be sick, but that excuse had worn a little thin. Completely transparent in fact. One party I went to I had to wait outside in the rain for ages and ages, waiting for a parent to open the door, while all the kids giggled and pulled faces at me behind the front windows. Another party I handed my present over to the "special birthday boy" and as he turned away I heard him say, "Yuk, yuk", put the present down and wipe his hands on his shorts; he laughed and everyone else laughed with him. Lots of dancing at those parties, but no one ever danced with me; I certainly never asked anyone to dance, because some things are just a complete waste of time. Two hours is a long time to sit in a corner watching people dance. Once I offered to be the record boy, to put new records on to keep the music going. "No way, don't touch anything, don't want you breaking anything. Or staining it." Much laughter followed. So, parties with their music and dancing were not my favourite thing.

Lisatoa told me that his dad was having a birthday party, though he called it a birthday celebration. Then he added, "Because he's gotten a year older", which I thought was probably obvious. I've noticed that lot of adults have birthday parties, even though they're not kids. I've also noticed that a lot of adults have a problem about getting older, about their age. I'm observant now that I'm a writer, and writers turn these seemingly insignificant observations into meaningful and perceptive insights. My insight is that worrying about your age is a silly problem to be worried about. It's not as if you can do anything about it. Well, except die I guess and that's not a solution I'd recommend. It's like that song Lisatoa's dad played where the man sings, "Ol' man river... he just keeps rolling." Paul Robeson was the singer and he said that the river is like time, you can't stop it, it just keeps rolling. My Oxford mum told me that the "literary technique" Paul Robeson used is called a metaphor. I think I might try to use some metaphors in my writing, can't hurt. My writing will then be littered with diamonds, every second word perfumed with sweet meaning and reading it will be the discovering of new horizons. I think there're some metaphors there. A metaphor is when you describe something, but you're really talking about something else. At least, I think that's what mum said. Like, it doesn't mean my writing is really going to have diamonds in it, I'm just trying to say how it will be really glittery and stuff. Mum went on to talk about similes, but I was still having trouble with metaphors. You probably are too. Thankfully, writers don't have to know this sort of stuff, we can just let the muse take over.

When I first heard that Paul Robeson record I knew the singer had to be a black man because his voice was so deep and wonderful, even when the song seemed to be about some bad things. Paul Robeson is dead now, but not completely when Lisatoa's dad puts that record on. He sings along with it too, and he sounds pretty good, not as good, but pretty good. I like that record, though not as much as The Beatles, The Easybeats, The Troggs or Herman's Hermit; I have very wide musical tastes. I kind of look forward to growing up, getting older, because maybe things will keep getting better, just like in my eleventh year that I'm telling you about. Eighteen'd be good. Or one hundred. Miss once commented in front of the whole class that something I said sounded, "wise beyond my years, almost philosophical." Maybe I could become a philosopher I thought, but at that stage I didn't think so, because I didn't fully know what it is they did. I mean, they couldn't sit around being philosophical all day long. I think my decision to be a writer is probably for the best. Though it is possible the philosopher stuff could help with my meaningful and perceptive insights, push them along a bit. Sometimes, I think there are just too many things in life for me to master, but I also think I'd like to give everything a bit of a whirl; it will be a long and hard journey, but ultimately rewarding as I peer around every corner, open every drawer and explore every avenue of unturned stones. I think there're some more metaphors for you there. However, I've got to say that I don't think this metaphor business is working for me, I just seem to be turning out stupid descriptions. It's better I relax, stop forcing stuff. I think I'll leave the metaphor game up to Paul Robeson. Though I still think I'd like to try other different things in life; different jobs, different countries, different people, different cultures, if for no other reason than different has to be more interesting than same. Seems there's so much ahead, but I guess it's one step at a time; a "journey of a thousand miles begins with the first step". (Not my metaphor.) Though, I don't see the necessity to walk the whole thousand miles, not when you could catch a bus. Or a train. Plane, possibly. Even a bike'd be better.

Well, if that last bit hasn't been me philosophising, then I don't know what is! Hmm, yes indeed, I might have been eleven, but clearly Miss might have had a point when she said I could be quite philosophical. I even suspect hmm is a thoughtful, philosophical sound. Hmmmm.

Gina once asked Miss how old she was and Miss said, "Oh, a lady never ever discloses her age." Gina then called out that she would be twelve later that year. Just like I was going be. I sensed that Gina and I probably had the same star sign. How nice is that! I knew for certain Stephan couldn't share our star sign because he was already twelve. So, there, I thought, take that! Both Gina and I are fifteen now, but our star signs have remained steadfast like the very stars themselves.

Lisatoa's dad was happy about his age. At his birthday party he beat his chest, raised his arms high and yelled out, "My name is Iosepha, I am forty, I have family, I have friends, and I am very happy." And it was a good party. That was a bit of a surprise for me. Lisatoa's dad had given me a small card with the birthday invitation on it. My insides squirmed a little bit when he gave it to me; it might have been Lisatoa's dad, but it was still a party. I had never been invited to a big person's party, but that didn't mean it was one of the "different things" I wanted to try. In the end, I didn't have a choice; mum would have made me go, but it was the look on Lisatoa's face that said I had to be there. When you have a friend, you have to do things for them that might be a little difficult. It should be a rule, a law even. I had no idea what to take along as a present, and Lisatoa wasn't any help because I don't think his dad needed a new football. I asked mum what I should get and she said, "Music, give him music." So, I bought him a record; it was second-hand, but didn't have any scratches on it and the sleeve was almost perfect. I bought him Ray Charles" *Modern Sounds of Country and Western Music*, which I know doesn't sound too exciting, but you wouldn't think that if you heard Ray Charles singing "I Can't Stop Loving You". I know that song because I played it a hundred times at home, which I know isn't the thing you're supposed to do with someone's present, but I was super careful and it was already second-hand.

I was leaving early for the party so I could help Lisatoa and his sisters, Moana and Linda, "make the place magic". Mum was in our loungeroom scrunching up pages from the local paper which she used to clean our windows. Every time she did this the gloves she wore would end up dirty and blackened from the newsprint, so don't ask me how it is that the windows got cleaned. Mum told me to wait a few moments while she got me something from the kitchen. I sat down in her chair to wait and on her side-table was the front page of the newspaper she had been using. The headline grabbed my attention: GREAT WAR VETERAN LEFT GNOMELESS. The article was about a World War One veteran: "70-year-old Clarence Davies, Clarry to those who know him, is completely heartbroken by the theft from his family home in Wallaby Crescent of his 17 garden gnomes, which he said was "the number of mates I had with me in the trenches. I even named each gnome after one of me mates, a sort of memorial. Loved seeing them each day, specially since Meg passed. What b****** steals a man's mates?"

When mum came back she was carrying the birthday cake. "Happy 40ᵗʰ birthday, Iosepha" the chocolate writing said. Cakes weren't the sort of thing mum usually made, but it was a very impressive job. I was just about out the door when I heard mum say, "I can't stop loving you." Suddenly I felt really warm all over, like I'd been dunked in a lovely bath. I kept walking to the party carrying my present and the cake. I wanted to start running, but that wouldn't have been very smart.

Dusk was falling when I arrived at Lisatoa's. It was one of those gentle evenings of soft warm air and you could hear the river whispering its secret messages into the night. I placed my cake on a long table that was already piled with all sorts of different food; it wouldn't just be a birthday dinner, it really would be a celebration, a banquet, a rejoicing. I helped set up the last of the decorations, then went with Lisatoa out to the front of his house which faced the river. When the guests arrived our job was to light, and keep going, the two bonfires stacked and waiting for us in cut-off forty-four gallon drums. This turned out to be a great job. If you're lucky enough to have ever been standing around a bonfire on a dark night, with the flashing lights, squeals and music of a nearby party you'll know what I mean; it's like you're part of the party, and you can dive right into it whenever you want, but you're also at a lovely remove from it. Once, years and years ago now, 1958 or even 1959, when I was three or four, dad had some friends from one of his ships over at our old home in Sydney. I guess it was a sort of party and mum was there chatting away with the wives and girlfriends. There was music playing (Dean Martin, Ricky Nelson), sometimes people dancing close together. I think I saw them dancing. I think. The smell of barbecue, huge bowls of curry and rice, the sounds of cutlery and plates, a glass breaking. An argument and tears, complete quiet, then a slow and muted clapping... like I said, it was a sort of party, and I was behind the lounge, at the party, but not at the party. I eventually fell asleep and woke up to a house of mess and my dad gone. It's an old memory, faded and blurred around the edges, and I keep it because I don't have very many. It doesn't make me happy or sad, it's just there.

There were a lot of people at Iosepha's birthday party. A few of them were from the church that Lisatoa and his family went to on Sunday. There were people from the local volunteer fire brigade, the football club, the friendly lady who served you at the grocery store and a group of young people with guitars who played music. Whenever they played their music Lisatoa and I would come in and listen. The men on the guitars had long hair like the singer from the Rolling Stones and the woman had long blonde hair like Nancy Sinatra. And Miss was there. You just don't expect to see your teacher at a party, having a giggling good time and dancing. And you don't expect her to wave like crazy when she first sees you and to then make you dance when the group did "Friday On My Mind". I didn't want to dance, I mean who wants to dance with their teacher? But I didn't get a choice, she took my right arm and before I knew it she was dancing in front of me. At first, I just stood there, not moving, but Miss just kept going, so I started to move a little. I guess I looked like a rusty, clunky robot and I felt that everyone must be watching me and laughing. But I really liked that song, "Friday On My Mind", and I just forgot about people watching me and laughing and got in to the music and dancing. I think I may also have sung along to the music. Then somehow the song was finished and I was sweaty all over and Miss said, "Three of those cheers for you, Ray."

When Lisatoa's mum came in carrying the cake I felt pleased that my cake was looking so special. If I'd been younger and more childish I might have called out, "That's my cake!", but this was a big people's party and I wasn't younger and more childish.

When Lisatoa and I went back outside to stoke the fires he didn't say a single word about my dancing with Miss, which I reckon shows you what kind of friend he was. If he had mentioned it, I would have told him that I liked it, which was true. Lisatoa and I went and stood beside the river and threw some stones in; it was nice to hear the soft kerplunk of the stones with the background sounds of a party finishing.

Standing beside the river, our two fires flickering behind us, reminded me of when mum and I first arrived there, the time Snarkey's truck had exploded into flames. "How come you and your dad were in the bush that night, the night that truck burst into flames?" I asked.

Lisatoa hesitated a moment, but he had nothing to hide, nothing to be ashamed of, so he explained how Snarkey ran the local garage, the only one in town, where he pumped petrol, did mechanical repairs, sold cigarettes to school kids, collected calendars where near-naked women recommended certain engine oils. "He's a small man with filthy fingernails and broken front teeth. He has bad breath," Lisatoa said. "He was using the river to dump old engine oil, like it was his own special tip. Supposed to pay to get it collected." Lisatoa went on to say how it was the hippies from the commune who were the first to complain, knew it was Snarkey. "But the local paper and police weren't interested in their complaints about hurting Mother Nature and ruining nude swimming. The hippies have never been real popular."

"My mum thinks they're okay."

"Then one morning my sisters and me went down to our jetty. Found an oil slick, filthy stuff, all around the canoes and wooden posts. Steps of the jetty all slimy black. Moana went and got dad. Dad was silent a bit, just stood there, then said, "The River God will make things right.""

Lisatoa also talked about other gods, not just the River one, like the god of the bush, the one of the mountains and another of the ocean. It was like he was giving a god to each of the big things in nature. I didn't know how that would work, like how big did something have to be to have a god? Could a mountain have a god, but if there was a small hill then it was out of luck? I think I accepted all this, with my philosophical spirit, because I knew Hinduism had a lot of gods and mum was good with that. I liked thinking that there could be forces out there that we couldn't see or understand. Which turned out to be just as well.

It was nearly twelve o'clock when people started to leave the party. Inside Lisatoa's house there was the after-party mess, but it looked happy, just a sign of a good time had. Iosepha thanked me for my present, telling me that it was just what he wanted, even though I'm pretty sure he couldn't have known or remembered what it was.

I felt really tired on my walk home. My clothes had the lingering smell of smoke from our fires and it smelt good. And I felt good. It seemed that parties with their music and dancing had become one of my favourite things. I think this is called "coming out of your shell", and yes, I know it's a metaphor, but that one seems okay.

When I got to our front gate I saw the twitch of the kitchen curtain and knew that mum had been waiting up for me. "Just on my way to bed," she told me. She gave a stretch and a yawn, but they weren't very realistic. "So, how was the party?" When I finished telling her, she went over to the cupboard beside our fridge, picked up a postcard and passed it me. "Right, see you in the morning," she said. I put the card in my pocket and told her I'd read it tomorrow.

The front of the postcard was a photo of a beach with people lying on the sand, surfers catching waves. Across the top it said, "Surfers Paradise." The back of the card was crowded with his writing, the last bit of which said, "This is where I'm living now, working in marine repairs, come visit, meet the others. Please!" I put the card in my bottom drawer, under my socks along with the others, and in the morning told mum I hadn't read it yet, was just too tired.

GARIDGE OF SURPRISES

You wouldn't have thought a dog with three legs could move so quickly, be so agile, be exactly like an ordinary dog. And that was a good thing for me to know. She could glide through the bush, avoiding all obstacles, even jumping when needed. However, she would never get so far ahead that she would lose sight of us. We had tried to find the dog's owner, all the time hoping we'd fail. At first we thought someone would be looking for her, or someone would recognise her and know where she was from. I mean, there couldn't have been too many three-legged whippets running around. But no one seemed to know anything; we got a lot of head shaking and "Sorry boys, can't help you there". There were no notes or posters stuck on shop noticeboards, no ad in the local paper. We were very happy.

Lisatoa called the dog Whippet. I could have thought of a zillion better names. But Whippet it was, because let's face it who was it who'd earned naming rights? However, there were those times when I felt it was Whippet and I who should have had the special connection. But it was Lisatoa and Whippet who were inseparable. She even went with us to watch him play football.

Lisatoa played in the under 12 rugby league team. His team was called the Badgers, which was a pretty stupid name if you ask me. Firstly, because we just don't have any badgers in Australia, and secondly because they are slow and lumbering animals. Lisatoa thought the Badgers was a good name, but then he was the one who called the whippet Whippet! This night the Badgers were playing the Condors, which makes you think that this naming business just goes on and on. When I first got to know Lisatoa I came to watch a couple of his practice games against other teams from his club. But this got incredibly boring because once people got to know Lisatoa they just got out of his way whenever he got the ball. Even his dad gave up watching the practice games. Competition games were better to watch, at least before people saw what getting in Lisatoa's way meant. I wished our town had some soccer teams, then my mum and Lisatoa could have come and watched me play and I would have impressed them just like Lisatoa impressed people, though my impressing would've been in a different way.

Badgers versus the Condors ended up being an interesting game. I say this even though I didn't much like rugby league, which was not something I broadcast far and wide. This game was interesting because the coach of the Condors, a young man with bushy red sideburns and moustache, must have known all about Lisatoa. So, throughout the entire first half he had three of his biggest players always close to Lisatoa, their job being to "stick like Tarzan's Grip" and to "smother" Lisatoa whenever he got the ball. If the plan looked good on the blackboard at training, it didn't work out in the game: three people watching Lisatoa, "like Tarzan's Grip", left a lot of other Badger players completely un-marked and free to do whatever they wanted. By the time the coach with the sideburns and moustache cottoned on to this it was all too late. When he finally changed tactics it unleashed Lisatoa. It was a slaughter.

The most enjoyable part of the game was the coach of the Con-dors. He started encouraging his players with yelling out things like, "Come on you Condors, swoop and dive" or "Fly Condors, fly" or "Get up, get up. Condors don't stay grounded". Quite often he would supplement his words of encouragement by walking along the sideline, frantically windmilling his arms, which I took to be his demonstrating how to take flight. Even Whippet looked up to watch. Towards the end of the game their coach became com-pletely silent, which I thought was such a pity because I was looking forward to even more ingenious Condor imagery. Later, walking home, Lisatoa said the Condors' coach was an English teacher at the high school we were going to next year. I sure hoped I wasn't going to be in his class.

We dawdled home after the game, Whippet the only one that seemed to have much energy, darting ahead to check things, then returning to us as if to report that it was all clear and safe to proceed. Then Whippet paused outside *Snarkeys Garidge and Machanical.* She sat down and tilted her head as if listening to something important, wouldn't budge even when Lisatoa called.

There was nothing interesting about Snarkey's garage, unless you counted the spelling. It was on the outskirts of town and out the front there was a small office with fibro walls and a flat roof with no guttering; it was where Snarkey took money for petrol and sold cigarettes. The large window was always grimy. Two petrol pumps, one shiny new, the other rusty and old, stood out front in the cracked concrete drive.

Behind the office was the large, corrugated iron shed where Snarkey did his work on the cars, not that there'd been a great deal of that since he'd been found syphoning off a little petrol from each car he serviced. Two huge doors at the side of the shed, where the cars got driven through when getting serviced, was where Whippet went.

Lisatoa called her again, but she wouldn't budge. Neither of us wanted to bump in to Snarkey, but in the front window of the office a large "Closed" sign was hanging so we thought it might be okay to see what Whippet was up to. We crept around the side of the office, not positive if the "Closed" sign meant Snarkey had gone home or if he'd just decided to stop selling petrol for the day and was in the shed. As Whippet saw us moving towards her, she pushed her way through a gap in the doors, tail disappearing inside. When we got to the doors, we could see that the wooden frames had warped at the bottom, giving enough space for Whippet to squeeze through. The doors were locked with a chain and padlock, but the chain was loose and Lisatoa could pry the doors open. He called out to Whippet, but got no response. At least it told us that Snarkey was unlikely to be in his shed. Without hesitating Lisatoa pushed his way through the doors. I peered between the doors and saw a large space of dark shadows, stinking of oil and petrol. Lisatoa's loud voice called me to come in and take a look. It was a place I would definitely not go in on my own, but I had two friends in there, so in I went, thus proving that those destined to later become writers and philosophers are made up of tons of courage as well as brains.

It took a few moments for my eyes to adjust to the lack of light. Several cars lined one side; they'd been there a long time, each of them sitting on flat tyres, door panels pocked with creeping rust, windscreens spiderwebs of broken glass. The concrete floor was oil-stained and slippery in places. One corner had a mountain of large cans, just like the ones I'd seen the night Snarkey's truck had burst into flames, dozens of them precariously stacked on top of each other. Moving closer to the cans I saw a deep hole that had been dug into the floor of the shed. Mounded beside the hole was a pile of dirt and broken concrete. Moving to the edge of hole, I peered in, knocking some dirt and concrete into it. A splash sound from the falling dirt and concrete made me look more closely. The bottom of the hole was black and viscous; Snarkey had found another way to get rid of his oil.

Whippet's excited barking got me to move away from the filthy hole. Around a corner of the shed, where a small and dirty window let in some smoky light, I saw Lisatoa and Whippet crouched around something. I walked towards them, moving past Snarkey's collection of calendars that lined a wall as if they were works of art hung in some small and crowded gallery. Getting closer, I could see that Lisatoa was patting and cuddling a dog, a kelpie with a large white marking on her head. While Lisatoa was doing this, Whippet was nuzzling the side of her neck.

"I didn't know Snarkey had a dog," I whispered.

"Neither did I," Lisatoa said. "And he shouldn't. He shouldn't have a dog, shouldn't be allowed. Look, look at this."

I followed the wave of his hand. The kelpie was tied around the neck with thick coarse rope, the fur on her neck rubbed away to skin that looked raw and sore in places. No food or water anywhere near the dog. I put my hand beside Lisatoa's and patted the kelpie's back and moving my hand around her chest I could feel the corrugations of her ribcage.

Lisatoa stopped patting the kelpie and moved over to the wall where the end of the dog's rope was tied around an engine that had long ago been removed from some small car. He began untying the rope. "What are you doing?" I asked, though it was pretty obvious.

"I'm taking this dog with us. Has to be done. It's also what Whippet wants."

"We're going to steal Snarkey's dog?"

"Yes! Steal this dog... save the poor thing. Look at him, got to get him out."

"Good," I told him. "Very good. Stealing. Excellent, excellent." This was exciting, very exciting. I thought of two budgies and that made it even more excellent.

Lisatoa handed me the end of the untied rope and I started to lead the dog away. I was officially a willing accomplice. I didn't think I'd touched anything, so no fingerprints. Leading the dog out it was as if she knew she was escaping, going to some place that just had to be better. When the dog looked up at me I honestly thought she was smiling. "You know, don't you? You're a clever girl aren't you? Clever, clever!" When I said those last words she stopped walking, sat down and looked up at me as if waiting for something more.

I was about to lead her out through the doors of the shed, show her some sunlight for the first time in a while, when Lisatoa called out to me, "Hey, come and take a look at this." I was keen to get away from the shed, courage does have its limits, but figured an extra moment or two wouldn't matter too much. When I turned around to go back the kelpie refused to follow. Couldn't blame her and no way was I going to pull on the rope, not with the raw skin around her neck. "I get it," I told her, "I wouldn't want to go back in there either if I was you. You really are clever, clever and stubborn." Again, she sat down and looked up at me, waiting for that something more. "Can you trust me for a second? Couple of seconds, then we're out of here." Just then Whippet appeared and the kelpie got up and started slowly walking back into the shed.

They were huddled in a group, just around the corner from where the kelpie had been tied. There were nine of them, standing shoulder to shoulder and facing outwards, looking brave and ready to resist anyone trying to break their ranks. They hadn't been too successful, however, because off to their right was a pile of shattered clay, shards of bright reds and greens, amongst which you could make out arms, legs and a head still wearing its green hat. A claw hammer sat beside the pile.

"Why on earth does Snarkey have this collection of little men, of elves?" Lisatoa asked.

"Haven't any idea, not a clue. Gnomes," I told Lisatoa, "not little men or elves. Gnomes." As soon as I said the word "gnomes" something stirred in the back of my mind, distant and unclear, but lingering and wanting to make itself seen.

When all four of us got outside it felt good to take a deep breath of fresh air. We moved away from Snarkey's garage as quickly as we could, just in case Snarkey should appear. We didn't leave the way we came in, not along the road, but chose to go around the back of people's houses, mostly hidden by small garden sheds, fruit trees and hedging. It doesn't always feel good to be doing something sneaky, something you don't want people to know about, but that time it felt great. I felt free, doing something I wanted to do, no matter the rules and no matter what some people might think. If stealing this dog from Snarkey was wrong, then so be it, because I was loving being wrong. My larrikin streak was coming along in leaps and bounds. I then thought how my mum and dad would understand and be proud of me; it was a strange and unsettling thought, one I'd not had in ages and ages, and I didn't know if I welcomed it or not.

We didn't get too far before we realised that we had a bit of a problem. Where were we going to take the kelpie? In the short term she could go to Lisatoa's and keep Whippet company for a while. Lisatoa was positive his parents wouldn't have a problem with that, it would just be one more dog to be added to two Pomeranians and one whippet. I also knew mum would let her stay with us. The problem with either of those choices was that people around town would eventually see her and word would get back to Snarkey and we wanted the kelpie to have complete freedom, not some brief escape.

When we got back to Lisatoa's we still hadn't solved the problem; that was something quickly done by Lisatoa's dad, right after we told him our story. He thought we'd done the right thing. "The hippies," Iosepha said. "They're certainly no friend of Snarkey's, not after all the oil that spoiled their part of the river. Probably still cleaning it up, so it would be fresh in their memory. And the bonus is, no one from the town goes to the commune, everyone steers clear. Yes, the hippies sound like the solution."

It was almost dark when we got to the commune. I'd been here once before when one of the hippies had asked mum to come for a visit. I think we were the only people from town who'd ever been there, which I thought was a little strange because I couldn't see what all the fuss was about. Sure, they were dressed differently to everyone in town, as was my mum most of the time. The men's hair was longer, but so what? When I'd been there with mum the hippies had been living in tents, but were building these wooden dome-like houses, no sign of fibro, concrete or bricks anywhere. Mum spent most of her time there talking to some of the hippies about Mahatma Gandhi, who mum said was one of the most important people in Indian and world history.

Later, after our visit, mum showed me pictures of Gandhi. He was this really little man, bald with thick glasses, which I thought was pretty inspirational because he ended up doing so many important things. While mum was talking about Gandhi I took a wander around the commune. The first thing I noticed was that they sure knew how to grow a lot of fruit and vegetables: tomato plants taller than me, heavy with fruit; grey pumpkins clinging to their vines; rows of peas and beans; avocado, lemon and orange trees newly planted; choko vines fighting passionfruit for ownership of a long stretch of lattice. Everywhere I went people were working away, looking up and telling me what a great day it was. I didn't find anything that could have added up to what the people in town were saying.

When Lisatoa and I got to the commune the first thing I noticed was how much things had changed. There were no longer any tents; these had been replaced by the domes I'd seen being built the previous time. There was now also a long building with a wide verandah that ran the full length of the front. A large fire was burning in front of the building, silhouetted figures gathered around it; two people hugging, someone dancing, people sitting cross-legged, another putting wood on the fire.

We didn't get much further before one of the figures in front of the fire moved towards us, a dark shadow that slowly coloured to life. "I hope you two aren't runaways. You're not are you?" We both shook our heads, though I could have told him I was a larrikin. "Hey, I think I remember you, you've been here before haven't you?" He looked me up and down, stared at my right hand that was patting the kelpie, then at my left arm, before adding, "I remember you, because I never forget a face." Straight away I knew that Lisatoa and I had come to the right place. He said his name was Walden, which mum later told me was probably not his real name and that quite a few people at the commune "take on new names because they're starting on a new life, a fresh start".

We told Walden the story of how we came to have the kelpie with us and what we were hoping the commune would do to help us. At first Walden was hesitant: "Don't want any trouble, well, any more trouble from the police or the people in town." However, when we got to telling Walden that the kelpie belonged to Snarkey he became quite enthusiastic, calling over somebody called New Dawn. "This is Dawn, but we call her New Dawn. New Dawn's a veterinarian nurse who spent two years in India looking after street dogs, before ending up here." New Dawn also said that she remembered my being here before, but that was because of my mum. "I wish your mum came her more often," she said, "such good karma she gives off. And knows so much." I agreed that mum knew a lot, and when I later found out what karma meant, I agreed with that too. New Dawn called the commune an ashram.

Before we left, New Dawn gave the kelpie a quick check over and when she felt her ribs she said she could use a good feed and a bit of exercise to firm up her muscles. "What a good looking girl you are," New Dawn said, "lovely brown coat and that beautiful big splash of white on your head. Beautiful girl."

Even if I hadn't known the time, that twitch of the kitchen curtain told me I was late. It had been a big day and as I ate my dinner I told mum all about it. She agreed that the kelpie would be taken good care of at the commune. When I was telling her about Snarkey's garage, the strangeness of his collection of gnomes struck me as even more odd. I asked mum why it was that the gnomes seemed to make me want to remember something, but she had no answers. It was like there was this little spark in the back of my mind and I was trying to make it clear and bright.

I had to wait three days into the school week before that little spark became clearer and brighter. Through the kitchen I went, checking the fridge for snacks, then into our loungeroom where mum was scrunching up pages of the local paper so that she could clean a couple more windows. Last time mum had been cleaning our windows, I'd read something about gnomes, gnomes that had been stolen from someone, not just a couple either, but lots of them. And Snarkey had lots of gnomes, some smashed up, hidden away in his shed. Had to be a connection, had to be. I told mum what I remembered of the article and asked when she'd last cleaned the windows. She said, "Always, always cleaning them. Never ending job," which wasn't at all helpful. What was helpful, however, was when she said try the local paper, go to their office and ask; "They can't have done too many recent articles on The Great Gnome Heist."

It was Friday afternoon when Lisatoa and I went to the office of the local paper. The person behind the desk looked to be about thirty. He had dark hair, quite long, covering his ears. He was dressed very conservatively, grey suit, white shirt, dark blue tie, which I knew wasn't unusual for someone behind a desk, but was kind of at odds with his Beatles' haircut. He stayed seated at his desk when we spoke to him and when he leaned backwards to answer the phone his hair fell away showing us ears that looked badly scared, sort of bulging. Later, Lisatoa said they were called "cauliflower ears", which made sense in a cruel kind of way. On the back wall there were framed pages from newspapers, all of them with different photos of the man who was now sitting behind the desk. One showed him holding up some football trophy, with the headline "One of Rugby Union's Best". Two other photos were of him arm in arm with a very tall and beautiful woman. In those photos his hair was short and his ears, as far as I could tell, looked pretty normal. In both of these photos his head was turned sideways to look at the woman as if he wanted to tell her something important, but she didn't appear to be listening because she was staring off at something outside of the photo. And in that very brief moment of looking at that photo I felt sad, because the lady should have listened to what he had to say and I just hoped that she didn't leave him, dump him, because later on he'd gotten those ears. Just because someone's beautiful and perfect doesn't give them the right to be mean to someone who isn't. I know they were only two silly photos, can't read too much into them. But still, that's what I thought.

"What is it boys?" he asked. "Hope you're not here about delivering the papers. Don't need any paper boys."

"No, no," I said, "it's about some stolen gnomes, an article about someone who had some gnomes stolen."

"You didn't steal them did you? Not here to demand a ransom are you? Come clean boys, admit it, come clean. Cops'll get ya and send ya up the river," he said, trying to sound like one of those gangsters in a late-night movie. He then burst into laughter. Lisatoa and I both remained silent while his laughter faded away. "No, not funny? Okay, yeah, I remember the article. Clarry had these gnomes, one for each of his war time mates, had names for them. Some mug nicked them. Every single one."

"Do you have Mr Clarry's address?" Lisatoa asked.

"Why? You're not going to irritate the old boy are you? Besides, can't give you an address, privacy and all that." He then stood up, puffed out his chest, hand on heart, and said in a deep voice, "And in addition, a journalist always, always, protects his sources." He then started laughing again.

"We've discovered the gnomes, their whereabouts," I said, which I thought sounded pretty good. Then I added, "And we'll give you the scoop when we've cracked this case wide open." Two could play that game I thought, but he didn't laugh, not even a grin, which I felt a little unfair because this was the first time I could remember my speaking out aloud and trying to be clever and witty. But he did give us the address and a copy of the article.

REVENGE OF THE GNOMES

Clarence Davies lived in Wallaby Crescent. Even if we hadn't been given the house number, it wouldn't have taken us long to find the right one. Out the front of Clarry's house were these cement stepping stones; I didn't count them, but was willing to bet there were seventeen of them, the exact number of gnomes stolen and the exact number of mates he had in the trenches in World War One. The stepping stones were scattered in small groups around the yard: some beneath a wattle tree, some beside a birdbath, two beside the letterbox and some lining the path to the front door. Each stepping stone had a name written on its flat surface, constantly reminding Clarry of what he had lost.

We were halfway down the footpath when a tall man appeared out of the shadows of the front verandah. He stood very straight, one arm resting on the verandah railing. His hair was white, thick and parted on the side.

"We've come about your gnomes," Lisatoa said. No point mucking around.

"Oh yeah," Clarry said, his voice wary and a suspicious look on his face.

"We know where they are," I said.

"That so?"

"Yes, and we know who took them," Lisatoa told him.

"That so?"

"But some of them are smashed up. The others are being held," I said, then added, "being held like prisoners."

"That so?" We stood there in complete silence, until Clarry slowly said, "I think you two chaps better take a seat on these front steps, while I grab two big glasses of ice-water."

Clarry was a very attentive and interested listener, not a single word from him until we'd finished. "All because I dobbed about his nicking people's petrol. Saw him doing it. Payback is what this is." Clarry then moved to go back inside his house. "Back in a sec, back in a sec," he said before he disappeared. It took a lot more than a sec before Clarry returned to us, more like twenty minutes, which is a lot of secs.

"Been on the blower, the phone. Got a couple mates, gnome mates if you get my drift. In a motorcycle club they are, twenty members, though the number keeps dropping because they're mostly like me: ancient. Some new members, young members, you know grandsons, some drifters, couple of big blokes, I mean *big* blokes who keep the riff raff out and stop any problems happening. This motorcycle club's called the Trenchers. Original name when it was just us World War 1 blokes. We were in the trenches together. France." I was wondering where this was going, when Clarry said, "Saturday tomorrow. If you're not busy, be at Snarkey's garage ten o'clock, see the Trenchers rolling in. Won't be a big deal, but worth a look." Clarry turned to go back inside, hesitated and told us, "Thanks, boys. I haven't got too many things that mean something to me. But those gnomes meant something. You boys ever need a drink of ice-water, or anything else I can help with, just give us a yell."

Sure enough when ten o'clock Saturday morning came about, Lisatoa and I found being outside Snarkey's garage was indeed "worth a look". We placed ourselves at a corner where we could get a view, and right on time ("Military precision," Clarry later told us) fourteen motorbikes pulled up on the road outside Snarkey's. They were big bikes, black and muscly. Three of them had those sidecars where a passenger could sit all safe and tucked away. Of the bikes with sidecars, only one had a passenger who just sat there, shiny leather jacket and a helmet that looked way too big. Sometimes the people on the motorbikes, the Trenchers, would rev their bikes, sounding like rolling thunder before a storm. It was then that the man from the newspaper turned up, large camera swinging on a cord around his neck, pen and notebook in hand. "Clarry give you an invite too I see," he said, before moving off. We could hear the clicking of his camera starting to do its work.

Most of the bikes, apart from the three with sidecars, pulled into Snarkey's garage and lined up at the petrol pump where they started revving their engines. A couple of the bikes began giving off these high-pitched, screeching sounds, just before their back wheels started spinning on the spot, tyres billowing thick blue smoke and a stench of burning rubber. Snarkey exploded out the front of his office, screen door flying open, to suddenly come to a halt as if he'd reached the edge of some sheer cliff. The bikes all fell silent, the rider of the first bike, the one at the pump, dismounted and said to Snarkey, "Petrol, good sir. Petrol for all of us." Snarkey would be busy for some time.

While the bikes had been making their noise and smoke, the three with sidecars had moved around the side to park outside the shed where Snarkey did his mechanical work, the shed where he kept a bunch of stolen gnomes and where a sad and neglected kelpie had once been tied. We saw the one sidecar passenger get out, take a quick look around, spot us and give us a wave. We both waved back at Clarry, who then leant back into the sidecar to take out a large pair of bolt cutters. Clarry hunched his leather-jacketed shoulders, stood as straight and tall as possible and walked towards the doors of the shed, swinging the bolt cutters as if he were some Viking warrior wielding a battle axe. It was an image that stayed with me and only a little diminished by the fact that the shed doors hadn't been locked, chain and padlock hanging loose. Clarry went through the doors, followed by the three motorbike drivers.

Just as they were closing the doors behind them I noticed that there was someone right beside me. Gina stood there, a curious look on her face, holding an old and scratched violin. "Practice," she said, "I'm learning the violin so I can be cultured. Important, my mum says. Got lessons at eleven."

"My family can sing," Lisatoa said. "Important singing, but it's not normal singing."

"That's okay, my violin playing's not normal either," Gina said. She smiled, then added, "So, you know why I'm here. What about you two? Saw all the bikes lined up for petrol. Heard the noise. Saw the smoke. What's going on?"

I gave Gina a quick account of Clarry and how Snarkey had stolen his mates the gnomes and how this was Clarry's way to get back at him. When I'd finished, Gina said, "My dad has special words for Snarkey, Italian words. But I'm not allowed to say them, or I'd have to go to confession. Busy enough there as it is."

Just then Clarry and the three bike riders reappeared at the shed doors, Clarry carrying four gnomes as well as his bolt cutters in his spare hand. One bike rider carried five gnomes and the claw hammer we'd seen beside the smashed pieces, while the other two were carrying small bags that bulged with whatever was inside. "This is just great, just great," Gina said.

Clarry climbed into his sidecar, along with his four gnomes which he placed on clear display beside him. It started to look awkward and crowded when the other rider tried to fit in the other gnomes. Clarry then looked up and waved for us to come over. Without any hesitation Gina moved off, leaving both Lisatoa and I feeling as if our roles in this show were in danger of getting stolen. Lisatoa and I followed, just behind Gina.

"Look boys," Clarry said when we got beside his sidecar, "I need you two to get in a sidecar each, not going too far, I need you in a sidecar holding some of the gnomes so that they're clearly on display when we join the line for petrol. Got to move now, military precision timing." Lisatoa started climbing into one of the sidecars and was already being given some gnomes.

"Gee, I don't know Clarry," I said, trying very hard to find an excuse that wasn't the truth, which was I was a little frightened of what Snarkey might do, frightened of drawing too much attention. At the same moment it came to me that I liked writing adventure stories, not living them, and that felt wrong, like I might miss out on something and regret it later on. "What if Snarkey..." I mumbled under my breath, thinking no one could hear me. Where had my larrikin streak disappeared to? Maybe it only appeared when no one was around, and that's not really what a larrikin is, you can't be a larrikin in private.

"How about I give you some of those Italian words that my dad used for Snarkey? That'd keep him away, scare him off." Gina said, then leant closer towards me and added, "Go on, you can do this." When I still didn't move, Gina started to climb into a sidecar, making exaggerated sounds as she swung her leg.

"Okay," I said, "okay. I *can* do this. *Want to*." Gina continued the swing of her leg, a complete arc that never touched the sidecar, probably never meant to. As I climbed into the sidecar, I looked at Gina and she had one of her smiles. My larrikin streak had just returned.

Three bikes and their sidecars slowly moved around to join the last couple of bikes that were still being filled with petrol; each sidecar contained a passenger holding aloft a bunch of gnomes. As we drove off Gina yelled, "Yippee, yahoo," then whistled loud and long. And she was going to violin lessons!

When we pulled up at the petrol pump, Snarky did a double take, let out a high-pitched squeal, and did a little jump, spilling quite a bit of petrol over his shoes. As soon as that happened one of the riders quickly came to stand beside him and pretended to have a very shaky hand that was trying to light a cigarette. Snarkey began waving his hands about, spilling more petrol, when the rider said, "Oops, forgot I gave up years ago."

When Clarry pulled up at the petrol pump he took off his helmet and smiled as if nothing was going on. He then turned to one of the gnomes he was holding and asked, "What do you think of this man who's about to fill our tanks?" He then leant over, putting his ear near the mouth of the gnome. "Oh, deary me, such language. You can't use those words. You're not in the trenches now. What's that you say? All right, I think you can say thief, cheat, liar, drongo, galah and fool. Not sure about, mongrel and scum. And I think that last one of yours needs to be modified to... let's see, how about bottom or bum?"

During all this Snarkey stayed silent, mouth agape. He only spoke when he'd finished filling the last tank, the one with my sidecar, and that was to tell the last rider the bill for all the petrol. It was quite a bill. My driver got off his bike, leaned in beside me and with one hand took out the two bags he'd carried out of the shed. "Smashed gnomes," he said, "broken mates." He then removed the claw hammer which had been tucked into his belt. As he was doing this Snarkey leant in towards me, all broken teeth and sour breath, and said, "I know you. How couldn't I, eh? Know your mother too. Two oddies." As Snarkey straightened, face all a sneer, I saw the claw hammer sail through the air, smashing the large window to his office. From just ahead of me Clarry called out, "That hammer can't seem to stop smashing things. And talking of things broken, that petrol bill is exactly, *exactly*, the price of replacement gnomes. Who'd believe it, eh?" When Clarry had finished speaking the man holding the two bags gave them a noisy shake and emptied them beside the petrol pumps.

Before Snarkey could utter another word, Clarry said, "Is that smoke coming out of your shed? I think you got a fire. You must be clumsy with fire, that truck of yours and all. Though I reckon this one could be because of those calendars, the girls set themselves on fire rather than have you look at them." Snarkey let out a string of swear words, before turning and running towards his shed.

I will admit it was very cool to be driven back to Clarry's home, a convoy of victorious Trenchers. I hoped Gina had stayed to see it. Clarry asked if Lisatoa and I wanted to stay for a barbecue and a few beers. He laughed when he asked. We told Clarry that we were heading home. Before we left, he again told us if we ever needed a drink of ice-water, or any sort of help, just give him a yell. "And most importantly if you have any trouble from Snarkey, any at all, just let us know. The Trenchers will ride again. That's a promise."

We never did have to call on Clarry or the Trenchers. But it was very nice to know we could.

I gave this section about Snarkey, Clarry and the Trenchers to Lisatoa's mum, Ethel, to read over. She said she really liked it, which I reckon is pretty high praise from someone who's written a children's book. I planned to show her more of what I'm doing. Nothing wrong with having a sympathetic audience.

DEEPER INTO THE BUSH

I never used to go very far into the bush behind our house, just far enough to get to my usual spots. I was the play-it-safe-kid who didn't want to become a headline in the local paper: Little Boy Lost in Bush. But that was before, before I developed my different streaks and before I had a best friend. Now Lisatoa and I were always going just that little bit deeper into the bush, pushing further each time. Each time we would quickly get to where we'd been the time before, and having gotten there it never seemed enough. We didn't want the familiar, the discovered territory, we wanted to see around the corner, to see if there was something new, something better. Most often it was more of the same, but occasionally there would be something new and different and that would be reward enough to go that little bit further the next time. So deeper and deeper we went. Whippet was our constant companion whenever we went into the bush. We once tried to leave her behind. She was asleep in Lisatoa's room, so we decided to close the door and let her get some rest. But there was no ignoring the howling cry she started up, could hear it miles away.

We followed the valley that had been made by the small, fast flowing river that joins the larger one that flows past Lisatoa's house. If there had been heavy rain the night before there would be the constant rumbling of rushing water and the gurgling tumble of a hundred small waterfalls. Most often the little river burbled along, pooling in places to then quietly slide over time-smoothed sandstone. The further we went the more wildlife we came upon. There was the startled group of drinking wallabies, splashing their escape across a shallow pool, to then stop and stare insolently back. We saw rosellas that screeched and squawked, a burst of impossible colour exploding from some ancient Moreton Bay before quickly disappearing into the never-ending green of a million trees. We stood still and watched the coiled iridescence of green tree snakes smoothly twining around low branches, their sleepy, blinking eyes telling us their life was slow and good. We saw huge lizards sunning themselves beside the glassy surface of deep rockpools while kookaburras threw their heads back and mocked us with their cackling laughter. Then there were the complete silences, so deep they felt to have a weight, suddenly broken by the loud drone of a million cicadas or some distant rolling thunder. Bush flies buzzed annoyance, their bulbous eyes, the intricate detail of their wings and their painful bite. And in the early evening, as we'd be heading home, there'd be the soundless flight of dark bat bodies crossing the sky, a haunting, mesmerising beauty. No wonder we went deeper and deeper. It is so, so good to not be the play-it-safe-kid. I think it's also good that Miss will be pleased that I'm sticking with this "setting the scene" business.

We were doing British explorers at school and Miss could get pretty excited about some of them. My favourite one was Percy Harrison Fawcett who was exploring the Amazon in search of the ancient lost city of Z. He was never seen again when he went searching the Amazon, looking for his mythical city, and no one knows what happened to him. It's a real mystery. Ancient civilisations, exotic and uncharted jungle, into the unknown, disappearance and mystery: easy to see why he was my favourite, even though Miss said he wasn't a very nice man in some ways. Miss preferred David Livingstone and when she was telling us how someone called Stanley found him in Africa and said, "Dr. Livingstone, I presume?" she got us to give "Three hearty British cheers." Lisatoa and I weren't in Africa or deep in the Amazon, and we knew that we were just two eleven-year-olds taking long bush walks. But there was still that little bit of me that slipped into the shoes of those explorers, imagined being them just for a few moments. I liked doing that. Usually, I'd be Percy Fawcett. Imagination is an essential part of being a writer (Obviously!) and I liked to let mine run free and wild.

At first it didn't look like much of an opening, just another hollow in the sandstone cliffs that lined the sides of the river. Would normally have walked right on by. But we didn't. One of those thunderstorms that we'd been having lately decided to come a little earlier on this particular day, and whilst that hollow on the cliff face didn't look like much it would have to do if we didn't want to get saturated. We huddled in the opening, the outside world darkening as if evening had set in early, the rain driving so hard that we started to get wet anyway. When rain began to run down the side of the cliff face, myriad rivers that found their way into our hiding spot, we pushed back as far as we could.

The storm quickly passed and the world outside brightened up smooth and fast, like turning up one of those kerosene lamps dad used to take camping. When we could see inside our shelter it became clear that it was more than just a hollow in the cliff face. Towards the back of the hollow there seemed to be an opening, a dark hole of a cave about three foot high.

Lisatoa bent down and cupping his hands around his mouth, yelled into the opening of the cave, "Hello. Hello." No reply, just a fading echo.

We decided to have a look into the cave, move into that opening, see what we could find. I know Percy Fawcett would have, so it naturally followed that I should. We began by sitting on our haunches and throwing one leg forward after the other. But that can be very awkward and very tiring. It's amazing how Cossacks can do their dancing. I gave that up and started to crawl along, which is a difficult thing for me to do; it's really a job that needs two hands. It's surprising how crawling can really hurt your knees. I didn't know how babies could do so much of it. Lisatoa, thinking aloud, wondered if snakes liked living in caves; it wasn't the best-timed thinking aloud. I wasn't scared of snakes, but sure didn't want to meet one in the cramped space of a cave. If I'd been at home I would have asked mum about snakes in caves; she had told me how when she was young she used to like watching snake charmers and their cobras, so she would likely have had a good idea.

We could hear Whippet's excited barking ahead of us. We crawled a little more, finding the going easier as the cave started opening up until we were finally able to stand. We found ourselves in a large space, a cave as big as our classroom, but with a much higher ceiling. A shaft of bright sunlight shone into the cave from a large opening in the roof. When Lisatoa moved into that shaft of light he could have been a character in one of those bible movies who is about to get the miracle he really needed.

We moved slowly around the cave, completely silent like wary trespassers. It was all so strange, so unexpected and so wonderful. It must have been how Howard Carter and Lord Carnarvon had felt about the discovery of the tomb of Tutankhamun in The Valley of the Kings. Of course, we did this in class with Miss; if you knew that Carter and Carnarvon were British, you probably would have guessed that already. Even if most stuff we did with Miss was British, we still learnt quite a bit, though some other countries would have been nice to have had included, like India, Samoa and Italy.

In the centre of the cave there was a fire pit, a circle of rocks, filled with ash and the stubs of sticks not completely burnt. A small mountain of cigarette butts next to one of the rocks. Lisatoa bent over and felt the ashes. "Hasn't been used for a while," he said, which I knew was something he'd seen in one of our TV shows. A canvas chair, the seat frayed and torn, faced the fire, a pile of wood beside it.

Neat stacks of wooden boxes, various shapes and sizes, lined the walls of the cave. A huddle of coloured glass bottles sat on top of one of the boxes. A small collapsible table leant against the cave wall, beside it several different piles covered with dusty khaki canvas sheets. I pulled aside one of the canvas sheets and found two billycans, one badly dented, three frypans, all blackened with use. There was a stack of tin plates, mugs and cups of odd colours and sizes. One of the larger mugs held an array of cutlery, some chopsticks. There was a large cooking pot, the sort you might set on top of the fire. Another pile was made up of cans of food. This person was awfully fond of Spam and vegetable soup. On top of the cans there were three different can openers. A couple of small hessian bags that contained what might have been rice slumped against each other, their contents spilt across the floor. Beside the bags there was a cluster of small tins. The labels of these were in another language, and only the addition of someone's rough handwriting told me what some of them were. There was curry powder, tinned two-fruits, rice pudding and lychees.

Further along, some shirts were neatly stacked on a wooden crate. I picked up the first shirt, a man's shirt, long-sleeved, a mottled khaki green and carefully folded. Even the buttons had been done up, as if the person cared about this shirt and it wasn't just something to scrunch up and shove away. Beneath the shirts were some folded trousers, same colour as the shirts. These too were neatly folded.

Moving along we found a small, dented tin trunk. An old padlock, rusted and left open, dangled from the lid. The trunk squealed when I lifted the lid, as if we were inflicting a short sharp pain on it. Inside, everything was tightly and neatly packed. There was a stack of paperbacks, all with the broken spines and creased pages of being well read. There must have been close to twenty books; the top few had names like *The Catcher in the Rye*, *All Quiet on the Western Front*, and *To Kill a Mockingbird*. Some of the other books were biographies and histories, really big books that would take ages and ages to read. I liked the sound of that *To Kill a Mockingbird*, decided to borrow it, somehow thinking it might be about getting back at people who do the putting down and mocking. And in some strange way, I was right. I was careful with the books. You shouldn't be rough with any book because you can't tell if there still might be something special about it, even if that something special is for someone else and not you. Before I went to school, I must have been four or five, I had all these *Winnie the Pooh* books and I just loved them; loved the characters, the stories and the drawings. They always made me feel happy and safe. Those books are really worn now, faded covers, cracked spines, loose pages, but I would still be upset if something happened to those old friends. I even had some Winnie the Pooh pyjamas and I loved them too; they were my lucky pyjamas. I've still got them somewhere.

We knew we had to head home soon, before it started getting dark. We would come back tomorrow, but before we left we decided to take a look at the cliff top above our cave. As we were leaving, I picked up *To Kill a Mockingbird* and took it with me.

Being on the top of the cliff, above our cave, was like finding yourself in a completely different world. We were above almost everything, some huge and ancient gums the only things higher. We could see the twists and curves of the river, water glinting diamond bright in the afternoon sun, the sandstone cliffs warm and honey-golden. An undulating canopy of mottled green stretched to the horizon. A flock of cockatoos wound along the snake curve of the river, white feathers a stark relief on the endless green, their raucous squawking eerily fading to complete silence. It felt as if we had been magically transported to some prehistoric time when the world was new. I bet Percy Fawcett had never seen anything better.

"Knew it'd be something great. We're like gods up here, like gods and we're looking at the world we made," Lisatoa said, his voice quiet and low.

We looked around a little more, found the remains of what might have been a hammock, now just some dangling cords and shredded canvas. We sat down on the edge of the cliff, Whippet between us, and took it all in. We talked from time to time, talking that at first needed no response beyond the listening. We wondered if we'd ever want to show this place to anyone else, share it. I said I'd share it with my mum and Lisatoa agreed, saying he'd share it with his family. Lisatoa went on to talk about his sisters and how they could drive him crazy, but how he could never get angry with them. He talked about his dad, how he's super strong, but super soft too. I liked hearing him talk about his dad. It didn't make me angry to hear about someone's dad, not anymore. It made me happy and it made me sad, but no, not angry anymore, even if there was a tiny hollow ache inside my chest. Lisatoa told me how his mum was the dreamer of the family, but also that special glue that happily stuck all five of them together and that's being super strong too. It is a good family that Lisatoa lives in.

Lisatoa already knew lots about my mum. Not much about my dad though. Never talked a lot about it before because... because... I don't *know* why. Embarrassment's not the right word, neither's shame or discomfort. Whatever the reason was, it wasn't there any longer. I told Lisatoa how my mum was born in India, in Bombay. Every time I said Bombay it sounded really exotic, like everything would be different, noisy, colourful and exciting there. Maybe I thought that because of mum's photos. One day I'm going to Bombay, I told Lisatoa, just to have a look. I explained how mum's family was supposed to be rich, something to do with exports. Didn't know how rich, but rich enough to send mum to Oxford and she was smart enough to go there and to do well. She met my dad when she was in London. They got married in Bombay. I'm still a bit short on details about that time. I also don't know how long it was before I came along; doesn't matter anyway. I told Lisatoa how I was born in Bombay. I didn't tell him how mum said it made her very happy, even if there was a bit of sadness there too. I guess everyone wants a perfect baby. I suppose I would. Mum tells me how I am perfect, just a bit different.

I told Lisatoa how dad worked for the British India Steam Navigation Company. Lisatoa said how that sounded important and impressive. Then I told him how my dad said he was the captain of the ship, which was a stupid lie, because he got found out so easily. I always feel a bit annoyed about that bit because I'll never know if he just got carried away or if it was a nasty sort of lie. I used to be certain it was a nasty lie, but a lot less certain now. Anyway, he wasn't a captain, he was an engineer's assistant. I told Lisatoa how some things went wrong with mum's family and after having a lot of money they ended up having very little at all. Mum said there was a kind of "poetic justice in that because we thought him the captain of a ship and he believed we were rich". I explained how I thought the names of the ships sounded magical and exotic, like they should be cutting across deep blue water, white wake trailing as they passed the lush greens of tropical islands, palm trees shading golden sand beaches. But when we lived in Sydney I saw some of his ships and they were nothing like that; they were all peeling paint, rusted sides and stinking of diesel, while the crew always looked sad and depressed, like they wished they could be somewhere else, but didn't know how to get there.

We sat on that cliff edge for ages. We didn't talk anymore, and it was completely peaceful to sit there in the silence.

INTRODUCING RANDOLPH

It was dark when I got home. I always tried to be home before dark because I knew mum got worried. She said she didn't, but that was just a white lie. When I came into the kitchen mum was sitting at the table reading the local paper, the one she said was full of nonsense, and my dinner was on the table. I was always tempted to say what fantastic timing, considering you weren't watching and waiting, but that would've spoiled the game we both knew we were playing.

We stayed in the kitchen after we'd washed up our dinner plates. It was a cloudy night, starless and very dark. For a while we just sat at our table staring out the window. Occasionally there'd be the sweep of headlights of some car driving home. We used to make up stories about the things we saw out of our window, stories about the lives of people in their cars, who they were, where they were going and what they were going to get up to. My stories were always about criminals who were on the run, their car boot full of stolen money, or maybe some hostage they'd locked in there. These stories always seemed to run out of steam, never develop into much. I now think they might have been the early training for my story about Tobias and his mother, because that one never seemed to run out of steam. Mum's stories about the people in their cars weren't much better than mine. They'd always be about a lady who'd been to the shops in the city and was driving home in a car full of the smell of the food and all the different herbs and spices she'd bought. The food, the herbs and spices would always be Indian, which was a pretty strong indication to me that mum was basing the lady in the car on herself, which I thought was a little unimaginative. Mum's stories rarely got beyond her laying the table for two. Sometimes I would push her to describe the dinner and the rest of the evening after it. I did this to encourage her, but she never got into it. I used to think a person who went to Oxford should have done a bit better. But now I'm sure it never had anything to do with Oxford or mum's ability to finish a story. In the end we gave up making stories about people in their cars and that was a good thing.

Instead, that night I told mum a story, not a made up one, about the cave Lisatoa and I had found.

"A hidden cave, you say, and a long way into the bush. Interesting. Any ideas who was there? Sounds like a man. But doesn't have to be."

I told her I didn't have an answer to her question, except to say that Lisatoa and I didn't think anybody had been there for a while.

We moved into our loungeroom with all its books, the "brain room", and we both settled into our chairs, turned on our reading lamps and sat there in our separate domes of light. Mum began re-reading *Wuthering Heights,* telling me how she found something new in it each time. I'd never read any book more than once and thought maybe I never would because there's so many books out there that I'd never get through them all, let alone some of them twice. Then I remembered *To Kill a Mockingbird* and went back to the kitchen to get it.

I came back with my book and began flicking through the pages. It was like I had two books in the one; lots and lots of handwritten notes in the margins as well as the novel itself. I looked at the handwritten notes because they seemed more real, more personal than the print, as if those handwritten notes were breathing and whispering to me. There was a person in those notes.

Lisatoa had an old photo of his great-great grandfather and he told me that sometimes when he stared at it he felt as if he was making some sort of contact, no clear messages or anything, but definitely some connection. Spirit speaking, he called it. Sounded a bit much at the time, not really possible. But there was something about those handwritten notes, because the more I flicked through *To Kill a Mockingbird* the more I got a feeling that there was a person there who needed something.

"Is that a library book, Ray?" Mum made me jump, I hadn't even noticed her leaving her chair to come and stand beside mine.

"No," I told her.

"Good," she said, "I thoroughly recommended making notes when you're reading, annotating it's called, but only if it's your book. Not fair to do it to a book someone else might read later on, like a library book." She leant over to look more closely at *To Kill a Mockingbird*. "I didn't know you had that novel. That's not your writing either. Great book, however. Quite a few messages in there for you. For everyone."

"We found it," I told her, "one of the books in the cave."

"Should probably tell the police about this cave of yours. No rush, but best to let them know. Maybe an escaped criminal used it as a hideout." She smiled and took *To Kill a Mockingbird* out of my hand and began looking through the pages. "And ah, we have a name," she said, "an owner." She handed the book back to me, and there it was in large print on the page beside the title of the novel. Don't know how I'd missed it. It was as if I'd been finding out about this person, things personal, before we'd been introduced, before I even knew his name. I didn't know anybody called Randolph MacGregor, but it felt better to have a name to go with the person I was finding out about. I asked mum if she had heard of anyone one called Randolph MacGregor, but she shook her head, then added, "But it's a Scottish name. Quite sure it's a Scottish name. You might ask Lisatoa's mum, ask Ethel, she's Scottish. Worth a try."

Monday morning I hung around the school gate waiting for Lisatoa to arrive; I'd ask him about Randolph MacGregor, then I'd try his mum in the afternoon. When he finally arrived I showed him the first page of *To Kill a Mockingbird* where Randolph Mac-

Gregor had written his name. At first it meant nothing to him, "I don't know anyone called Randolph."

"Okay, okay. I think I'll ask your mum this afternoon, see if she knows."

"If you like, but I've never heard mum or dad mention a Randolph."

"Yeah, but I'm interested in the last name, the Scottish name. She might know that," I said.

"Last name? Show us again."

"Randolph MacGregor," I said. "The last name, MacGregor, that's the one your mum might recognise. MacGregor, a Scottish name." A group of students was passing us, slowly heading off to class when Gina broke away to stand beside us.

"MacGregor! Whoa, of course, of course," Lisatoa said. "It's Alex, it's got to be, just has to be. Alex's name is MacGregor, Alex MacGregor. Incredible, incredible, Alex's dad. Couldn't be anyone else. He died about a year ago? Not long before you came here. If it's Alex's dad, he died a year ago, maybe a bit more."

Gina was nodding her head, "That's right. Lung cancer. Alex's dad? Lung cancer. Died of lung cancer. Papa, dad, gave me a long, long lecture about smoking. So, I remember it was about a year ago. Alex was okay before that happened. Sort of. Not always good, but sort of." That was a side of Alex that I'd never seen. "I remember the time," Gina continued, "because I was taking my brother to Cubs, you know at the Baden Powell Scout Hall, and there was this man from the local bush fire brigade holding Alex by the scuff of his neck. Alex was squirming like crazy and yelling stuff like, "I hate uniforms. Got to burn uniforms, hate 'em all." And sure enough he'd taken all the uniforms out of the hall and had set fire to them. Lots of smoke, not much flames. My brother had just turned six, that's how I remember when it was. He burst into tears. My brother, that is. And I know tons and tons more. But you have to tell me what you're up to."

Lisatoa said that he knew tons and tons too, and told her about the cave, about *To Kill a Mockingbird* and Randolph MacGregor's name. I didn't think it was fair that Lisatoa did all the telling; we should have shared it, with me doing most of the telling.

"So, that's where he was," Gina said, "people thought he just disappeared. But he was hiding in the bush. There was a bit of a search for him in the bush, but that soon stopped. Nobody had any idea where he could be."

"Why did he go away then come back?" Lisatoa asked. "And then he died a couple of weeks later. Should have been in hospital or something."

"We had a cat that got sick and it just disappeared one day," Gina said. "My mum loves cats. As much I do. Mum's cat was called Top Cat, just like in the cartoons. It was her lap-cat. Mamma loved Top Cat, even if it did leave hair everywhere. Anyway, mum said Top Cat was super smart and affectionate and when she got sick and was going to die she just went off into the bush. Mum said it was because Top Cat didn't want her to see her suffering and to get upset. Mamma cried like anything anyway."

We were all quiet for a moment until the bell. I knew Gina Fontana wasn't only smart at maths. It was clear that she had a philosophical streak without even trying. When she turned to leave she gave me a smile and though it was a sad sort of smile it was still nice. I didn't get a wink that time, because it wasn't the sort of conversation where a wink would be the right sort of full stop. If you know what I mean. Besides, I didn't want to be greedy.

We set out early that Saturday, moving through the hazy light and dim shadows of early dawn. It was around eight when we got to the cave, which was good because it would give us plenty of time to check everything out. After today we would tell the police, or whoever, what we had found.

Whippet was the first inside the cave and went straight over to the trunk as if knowing this was where we should start. Beneath the paperbacks there was a package wrapped in waterproof canvas and tied with two ribbons, one a red tartan, the other a green;

they reminded me of the hair ribbons Lisatoa's mum used. We slowly unwrapped the package and found lots of packs of different cigarettes, all with strange names and writing in some Asian language. One of the packs was open, and the cigarettes felt damp and smelt like rotting grass.

There was a small box containing a collection of bottles, the sort you would get cough medicine in. Most of the labels were in a language similar to that of the cigarettes, but some were in English: there was a bottle, nearly empty, of pethidine, a larger one of codeine and two of valium. There were lots of empty bottles. I recognised the pethidine and knew what it was for because when mum dislocated her shoulder the doctor had given her some. "This'll take the edge off almost anything," Dr Petroni told her, "but be sure to only take the correct amount when you're back home. It's addictive." Maybe mum didn't have the correct amount, because I was in the surgery when Dr Petroni put her shoulder back in and she screamed awfully loud.

Then we found the gun. It sucked in all our attention as it sat there in its leather holster, its grip sticking out, waiting for a hand to wrap around it. My cowboy shows told me that guns were supposed to be cool, guns were necessary, they protected people and they were both good and bad; such was the power of a gun. I had learnt all this from a thousand hours of *Rawhide, Bonanza, The Rifleman, Tales of the Texas Rangers* and a dozen other cowboy shows. But this felt different, it felt so much more than anything I'd ever seen while seated in my chair as thirty minutes of black and white adventure spooled before my rivetted eyes. Neither of us put out a hand to touch it, let alone pick it up. Yet neither of us looked away.

The gun was leaning against a small box as if guarding it, a cold steel sentry. I liked it a lot better when we'd been finding tins of Spam and paperbacks.

THE DIARIES

I gently laid the gun aside, as if it was something sleeping, something I didn't want to awaken. I lifted out the small box that it had been leaning against. It was made of wood, slightly larger than a shoe box, cracked and warped all over. Inside there were three different sized notebooks; they were diaries with the same handwriting as in the margins of *To Kill a Mockingbird.*

Each diary had the year 1959, 1960 or 1963 on the spine, originally in gold lettering, but now faded and flaking away. Other years must have gone missing. The 1959 diary was full of writing, while the 1960 one had very little, but lots of photos, most of them stuck together by time and humidity, waiting to be gently pried apart.

The diary from 1963 was something else. 1963 had dark pencil sketches and some of the pages were scored and torn through from pressing too hard. Lots of the sketches had been scribbled over, obliterating whatever had been drawn there. Most of the writing was chaotic, with half-finished sentences, swear words, random references to "my saviour", all barely legible. There was the occasional page that was clearly expressed and written as if the person was able to take a good deep breath and settle down.

I went back to the first diary; it started with some grumbling about food: "completely tasteless, always the same. Miss home cooking. Imagine that! Still, can't say there ain't tons of it. Never go hungry in this man's army. And you get all the ciggies you want." The writing went on to say how Randolph MacGregor had been in the army for four years and that he'd "gotten fed up to me eyeballs" with doing nothing but pointless drills.

We kept flicking through the pages, reading a sentence here and there and sometimes whole entries if they looked interesting. Occasionally Randolph would mention his wife, "me beauty", but never so many times that you thought he was missing her.

It was near the end of the 1959 diary that we came upon his first mention of Alex. Maybe there'd been lots of earlier mentions and we'd just missed them in our skim reading. There was a heading, underlined twice, that said, "LETTER TO ALEX, ROUGH COPY". It was quite a long rough copy, but some of the lines jumped out at me. They jumped out at me and have stayed ever since: "Remember you're the BIG MAN now," Randolph wrote, which was quite a call considering Alex would have been about five. He went on to say how "BIG MEN help out around the house, they brush there teeth, pay attention in school so's you don't end up like me. But most off all BIG MEN must always always remember that there daddy loves them and I miss giving you a kiss an cuddle each night." I stopped reading there, the words stung and for a few moments I couldn't go any further. It was like I was looking in on some special moment, a private moment where someone was showing how hearts work. But now that that person was gone, I wondered, did that mean the love had gone too? I wondered if he got to send those letters. Hope he did. I thought about how important those letters could be to Alex. Letters like postcards, I thought, letters like postcards.

Further on there were a lot of blank pages, but the ones written in talked about "deployment" to Malaya, because there was something called the "Malayan Emergency". Randolph seemed to be excited about this, "some action at last, no more cleaning barracks and bloody mindless drills!"

The 1959 diary ended with another rough copy of a letter to Alex promising to make "you and your mum as proud as punch of me. Probably get a metal, that's what me mates are thinking we'll get a metal and that should show everyone don't you reckon?"

When I again opened the 1960 diary some of the photos came sliding out. They showed groups of men in a jungle camp, long pants, singlets, holding machine guns and grinning ear to ear, standing in a drift of campfire smoke, frozen forever in black and white. They looked like a bunch of kids, all excited by a holiday adventure. I had no way of knowing which of them was Alex's dad. The writing was all about finding the "commies", tracking them down like it was some game. Some complaints began to creep in: "bloody mozzies, big as bees, sick of tin food, except for Spam... diarrear and no bloody toilet paper." There was another rough copy of a letter to Alex, making everything sound much better than any of the diary entries. He told Alex how "it's really tops out here with me mates. But nothing's as tops as things are going to be when I get back to see you my Big Man. Miss you so, sooo much. Be bonza to see you again, bonza, bonza."

I turned to face Lisatoa and stared at him. Then out of nowhere, no idea at the time where they came from, I started to cry, nothing loud and sobbing, but there was definitely the slow slide of tears.

"There's just so much here," I said to Lisatoa, "just so much in these postcards, so much sad stuff in these postcards."

"Letters, Ray, not postcards."

I had only ever had a hug from my mum or my dad, but I sure needed the one Lisatoa gave me.

A little later we looked at the last photos. The men were still around the jungle camp, but they no longer looked as happy, and even in the black and white photos you could tell they felt hot and dirty, hungry and sad. They looked like skinny young men who just wanted to go home. I didn't want to think why the photos now had less men in them. However, the next photos told me why. Three stretchers holding bodies, covered in cloths. They were only black and white photos, small enough to hold flat in the palm of your hand, but they somehow seemed bigger and heavier and for a moment, just a moment, I could feel the weight of jungle heat and smell the sweat, the fear and loss. Maybe it hadn't always been so good for Percy Fawcett.

The writing on the back of some of the photos talked about someone called Lenny, who'd died. "He was me best mate... take a bullet he would." Lenny hadn't died fighting "the commies, there everywhere, everywhere and nowhere", he'd died of some "tropical disease, vomited and diahareaahed and sweated his life away". One of the photos was taken either early morning or late evening and it was of the jungle; it was a wall of looming trees and impenetrable undergrowth, dark and threatening. On the back of that photo was the writing: "We refused. Crazy suicide. All seven of us. Told the brass to do it. Court Martial they said. Ha!"

We again picked up the diary from 1963. Maybe it would make a bit more sense now, but it still wasn't easy to read. It looked like 1963 had been written in our cave. In half-finished and jumbled sentences Randolph explained how he "escaped" there with his "Saviour". Lisatoa's thought Randolph had turned all religious. We worked out that he'd stayed in the cave for at least six months, possibly even more. Towards the end of the diary some of the pages had a spray of red dots across them, as if someone had sneezed with a mouthful of red cordial. Towards the end of the diary we worked out what Randolph's Saviour was. The Saviour "promised me relief. Fully loaded, but I haven't got the guts. Nothing new there."

Both Lisatoa and I had seen enough. It was beyond us. We needed to take this to people who'd know what to do. If there was anything to be done.

TAKING RANDOLPH HOME

We could have taken the diaries to the police, or my mum or Lisatoa's parents. Either would have been a safe and good idea. Just not the perfect one: MacGregor diaries belonged to the Mac-Gregor family and then it would be up to them to decide what it was they wanted to do. We knew where Alex's place was, everyone knew. Ethel, Lisatoa's mum, had once taken us there to "see a bit of Scotland".

Alex's dad, Randolph, had worked in the local timberyard, be-fore he'd joined the army, both well before I'd come to live in the town. Randolph built their house and that was why everyone knew where the MacGregors lived. Their house was one of the few two-storey ones in the area and it was made up of different types and cuts of timber that had come from Randolph's work. The front of the house was like a log cabin you might see Davy Crock-ett walk out of. One side of the house was made out of large cuts of sawn timber, the sort used in slab huts, and the spaces between each piece were filled with what looked to be a mixture of mud and grass. You could actually see stalks of grass sticking out all over the place. The other side of the house was made up with hundreds of pieces of wood that would normally go into making a paling fence. The palings were alternately painted blue and white, "Scottish colours", but they made me think of the surf. There were two front verandahs, one at ground level and a second one above it on the second floor. Railings on the ver-andahs were made from small trees that had been cut for the purpose and you could see how they were thicker at one end, tapering towards the other. You could also see that Randolph had left the bark on the railings and that it was peeling off in different places. The floor of the upstairs verandah had a bow in the middle, quite a big bow, and you'd have to wonder if it was com-pletely safe. Two large upstairs windows looked like staring eyes above the curved smile of the dipping verandah. In the front yard of the house there was a flagpole as tall as a telegraph pole, but not as thick, and flying from the top, as big as a double-bed sheet, was the Scottish flag. I know it was the Scottish flag because it was the last thing Lisatoa's mum had explained. That was the only time I had been there. People might have laughed and shaken their heads at the house Randolph built, and it's true that it was kind of crazy and higgledy-piggledy, but I thought it was wonderful. I mean, I lived in a three-bedroom fibro house, so why wouldn't I think it wonderful? It's just lucky that my particular three-bedroom fibro house had some very special things about it.

Lisatoa and I paused outside the front of the MacGregor's house. The first thing I noticed was that the flagpole was still there, but there was no longer any large Scottish flag flying from it. The front of the house still looked like Davy Crockett's log cabin, and the upstairs verandah had the same sagging appearance, but the railing had gone. The upstairs windows were boarded up and the painted fence palings that made up the side of the house had faded, no longer the bright blue and white of surf. It made me a little sad, as if the place had surrendered parts of what it had once been. It was a house that had lost things.

Standing there, diaries in my backpack, we didn't know what to do next, how to go about things. We had hiked deep into the bush, discovered and explored a cave, but this seemed the hardest. We didn't know who would be in the house. We'd never seen Alex's mum, but assumed she would still be living there. We didn't even know if Alex would be there, or if he had to stay at the "special" school he'd been sent to.

In the end we just walked down the path at the front of the house; play it by ear we told ourselves, can't make a definite plan for something like this. Maybe we'd simply tell Alex's mum how we found a cave where her husband, Mr MacGregor, had stayed for a while and how we found these diaries. Then leave. I guess.

At the front door we stood on a brown doormat that said "Welcome." A brass doorknocker, a small lion's head with flowing mane, was fixed in the middle of the warped plywood door. It was Lisatoa who finally grabbed hold of the doorknocker. It took a while for someone to answer, but we could hear movement inside and a raspy voice telling us, "On my way, just a tick."

The door slowly groaned and squawked open, the bottom dragging along the floor of the hallway, further scoring the arc in the green linoleum. "Good afternoon laddies. What can I do for you?" She was a short woman, no taller than me and her voice sounded deep and rough, like she might have a bad cold. I thought she was somewhere in her sixties, though I was never any good at older people's ages. Anyway, I remember thinking she was pretty old to be Alex's mum, but figured some people have young parents and some people have old parents and the age thing probably wasn't the important bit about parenting. "Collecting for the Scouts are you? Hopefully, you're industrious lads looking to earn a bob or two doing odd jobs? I could use you for that," she said, waving her arm across the front yard. For the first time we noticed that the yard was a bit of a mess, overgrown with weeds, sticky heads of paspalum standing high.

It was Lisatoa who responded, "No, no we're not Scouts. Are you Mrs MacGregor? Alex's mum?"

It took her a bit to answer. She folded her arms across her chest. Her arms were almost as big as Lisatoa's dad's, but there wasn't much muscle there. Some of her fingers were yellow at the tips, a warm yellow tinge. "I'm Mrs MacGregor," she finally answered, "but not Alex's mum. No, no, I'm his granny. Why do you ask? Is there something you want, something I can do for you? Not that I'll do it, mind you. Probably won't in fact, but you might as well give it a go." I didn't think she was sounding at all friendly or helpful, but when she smiled, wrinkles showing at the corners of her mouth, it was a nice smile, easy, warm and real.

"Could we see Alex's mum?" She remained silent, so I added, "Please," in a sort of begging, pleading voice. It's one that sometimes worked with mum, more often than it probably should.

"Nope," she said while shaking her head as if she'd swallowed something really bitter. Her shoulder length hair, grey with some lingering black threads, swung from side to side. It did not look like very clean hair. But then that nice smile popped up again, as if she was pleasantly amused.

It was Lisatoa who took up our case. "Okay, he said, "we know we can't see her because she's not here, not right in front of our eyes. But is she inside? Is Alex's mum inside?"

"Sorry boys. She hasn't been here for years," she told us, then quietly added, "Thankfully." Hearing that was something we hadn't expected, we just assumed Alex's mum would very conveniently be waiting for us to turn up. And we were confused by the "Thankfully". Nobody said anything for what seemed like ages; we were stuck in the awkward silence, run aground on some obstacle we couldn't see.

Seemed there was only one thing to do. "We found stuff that belongs to Mr Randolph MacGregor, lots, important stuff," I blurted out. I didn't think about it, just said it. "We found things that belonged to him. Things that must get to Alex."

"Did you now?" she asked. She tilted her head down a little and looked as if she was carefully thinking things over. There was no sign of the smile we'd seen before.

"We found this cave, deep in the bush, and it had lots of his stuff in it," Lisatoa said.

"And books. Lots of novels, but not just novels. There were his diaries there. And we've got them with us now."

"A cave, eh? Well, well, well. In the bush, eh? Wouldn't have picked that. Or the diaries, never in a million years," she said. "I'll be honest boys. I reckon you think you're doing the right thing, bringing stories and diaries here, I get that. I'm not stupid, so I get it. But I don't like opening old wounds. Hard enough as it is, with

Alex and all that. You know what I mean when I say, opening old wounds?"

"Sure," I told her, "it means making something hurt all over again."

"That's right."

"But what if there's stuff that makes those wounds get a bit better, what then? There's good things in the diaries, not all of it, but there's good stuff," I told her. Again, I thought about what the diaries said about Alex.

"Easy for you to say. Pandora's Box, boys, Pandora's Box. Know about that too, do you?"

"Yes, yes. But it's not all bad stuff, not by a mile. And it's not right to keep the lid closed," I told her.

"Well, aren't you the clever one?"

I reached into my backpack and took out one of the diaries, opened it and held it in front of her. She reached out to touch it but withdrew her hand as if it might bite. She started to slowly drag the door closed when I turned the diary around and began to read aloud. "Some days I think I should go back, back to be with Alex, things to fix back there, things broken by me and not by me, but then... I need home..." She stopped closing the door, stared hard at me. My reading trailed away.

"You better come in boys. I think you better come in. How about you call me Mrs M?" And the door groaned and squawked wide again.

Later, Lisatoa asked me about my taking the diary out and reading it aloud. "You had that bit picked out to read, didn't you? Smart thinking."

I shook my head and told him how I hadn't planned it at all, just a spur of the moment thing. At first he didn't believe me. "No, I just picked one of the diaries. Had no idea which one it was, could've been any of them. Just opened it up, started reading."

"Hmm," said Lisatoa, "forces at work."

INSIDE THE HOUSE

"You better come in boys. I think you better come in. How about you call me Mrs M?" She then looked down at Whippet and said, "Bring your lovely friend too, as long as she's house-trained. She house-trained?" Mrs M didn't wait for us to answer. "I used to have a dog, beautiful kelpie. Was my friend. Miss her, I do." She shook her head and was quiet a moment. "Oh, well," she said. "Can't seem to get used to losing things, you know, things you love." She finished talking and slowly walked off. We followed her, moving along the hallway dimness, floorboards creaking under faded linoleum. Family photos on the walls, three closed doors, an intricately designed pedestal holding a flowerpot filled with maidenhair fern. Mrs M stopped at a one of the photos. "That's all of us," she said, "the whole clan. Three generations." I looked at the photo, fifteen or so people huddled together: toddlers, teenagers, adults, grandparents, all with grins stretched across faces, standing there in their Sunday bests.

The kitchen was small, two of the walls lined with open shelves, neatly stacked with cans and packets of food. I saw a couple of cans of Spam. A fruit bowl sat in the middle of a round table, its red laminate top lifting at the edges. A cream-coloured fridge hummed. Everything was worn and old, but nothing was out of place and everything spotlessly clean. She told us to sit down, "Take a load off your feet, lads." She took out two plates, one red, the other white, and put them in front of us with some chocolate biscuits. She asked if we wanted a cuppa, and we thanked her, but said we were fine.

More photos were hanging on the wall beside the fridge, my attention drawn there because four of them were turned around, only their cardboard backing showing. Mrs M saw me staring. "Turn them around when I need a chat. Otherwise, I just let them rest all nice and quiet. Best for them. And for me." She turned the top photo around and there was this young boy all dressed up in a kilt, trying to hold a set of bagpipes almost as big as he was. "Seven Alex was. The world all stretched out in front of him. That's his dad beside him." The next photo was of a young man standing beside an old Holden, one foot on top of the wheel and an arm draped across the roof, a smirk on his face. "Randolph's first car. Just look at his face, thinks he's the bee's knees, the ant's pants." She shook her head. "And speaking of animals," she reached for the bottom photo and turned it around. Lisatoa got out of his chair and stood in front of the bottom photo. I was pretty certain he was thinking the same thing as me, that the dog in that photo looked very familiar. Sure it was a younger dog, but there was definitely a resemblance.

I was just about to say something when Mrs M turned around and sat down on one of the kitchen chairs. She was quietly crying. I wasn't used to grown-ups crying (still not) and it made me feel all awkward and funny, like do I give her a hug or look the other way and pretend it's not happening? "Sorry boys, silly old duck I am. Just a bit fresh that one." She brushed the tears aside, took a jagged, deep breath. "Just disappeared one day. Must've been early morning when I let her out to do her business. Must have wandered off, got lost. Which is really strange, because she was really smart." She paused a moment, and in a voice that was a little too loud said, "Right boys. The diaries. Let's have them. I can do it. Let's have them."

When we took out the diaries and placed them on the table they looked older and more worn than they had in the cave. Also, a lot bigger and heavier, more important. Mrs M picked up one, turned it over in her hands before putting it back down. "Might take me a bit of getting around to boys. If ever." I remember feeling a little disappointed, like I wanted her to race through them all then and there so that she would know what we knew. We sat there for a while, the occasional crunch of biscuit the only sound, until Mrs M said, "Give me a week, boys, give me a week, then come back for a chat. How's that sound?" A week sounded an age, but we nodded. "Good. But mum's the word until then, okay? Mum's the word. Promise?" We crossed our hearts and she was happy with that.

As soon as we were away from Mrs M's house, I said, "That dog of Mrs M's, that photo, do you think...?"

"Got to be, just has to be. It's like the gnomes, the gnomes and Snarkey." Lisatoa said. "And only one way to know for sure."

At the commune it was Walden who first moved towards us, arms wide, giving each of us a hug and saying, "Welcome." In hurried and jumbled sentences we told him the story about Mrs M and what we think Snarkey might have done. "There's just no end to that guy is there? I don't like to think the worst of anyone, but that Snarkey, I tell you." He then told us that New Dawn was at a nearby commune where they were "doing wonders with chickens, free range, free as a bird you could say, lots of eggs and fertiliser, but no murdering". New Dawn had taken the kelpie with her, but would be back in a few days. Walden said how it would be hard to give the dog back, "But all creatures need to be where they belong, where the vibe's strongest. That's *if* you're right and that's where she belongs. *If*."

Lisatoa and I spent a long week waiting to go back to see Mrs M. Each night I read Randolph's copy of *To Kill a Mockingbird* by Harper Lee. It sure had a lot of Randolph's handwritten notes in it and even though we didn't have his diaries anymore it was a way of keeping a bit of him nearby. In the end I got to learn about the characters in the book and the character who had read it. It was a good deal. I think I might have also liked that book because of the name of the author, it sounded different and cool. I think that if I ever came to write a book that was going to sell millions and millions of copies, I would make up a different name for myself, something like Garrison Penhalion or Scout Emerson or Lee Magnum Fullerton, or something else, something a bit better than Ray Williams.

There's this bit in the book when this character called Atticus (another cool name) talks about understanding other people. I copied it down: "You never really understand a person until you consider things from his point of view... until you climb inside his skin and walk around in it." When I was eleven I thought it pretty good advice. Still do now that I'm fifteen. And probably still will when I'm a hundred and fifteen. In the end I think it was a book that showed you just how horrible people can be, but also how good, how great people can be. *To Kill a Mockingbird* might be made up, but it's also true.

We spent the week at school concentrating on English kings and queens, especially Elizabeth 1, who Miss was especially keen on. Our book only had eight pages, out of a couple of hundred, on the Elizabethan Age, but it was where we spent most of our time, all the other kings and queens barely getting a mention. We quickly looked at Shakespeare, the Spanish Armada ("Three hearty British cheers for the English Navy!"), Sir Walter Raleigh and Sir Francis Drake. There was a colour drawing of Drake's ship, The Golden Hind, which looked awfully small to sail around the world in. Lisatoa said it was a lousy drawing and that he could do a lot better.

When Miss said that the age of Elizabeth was the time England began to conquer different parts of the world, Gina called out (she never put her hand up) asking if we could study the Romans because they were Italians and they conquered *all* the world. Miss said, "Definitely not. Besides Britain conquered more, much more."

"More than *all* the world, Miss?"

"The Romans most certainly did not conquer *all* the world. Just a bit of it," Miss said.

"Was Britain one of the bits the Romans conquered, Miss?"

"Right, that's more than enough history for the time being. History books closed and away under desks. Maths books out," Miss said, sounding quite sharp and firm. I could see Gina grinning. She could look quite mischievous at times. And a bit pretty.

THEY'RE HOME NOW

The sun was just rising that Saturday morning when Lisatoa and I turned up at the commune. There were already several small fires burning, people moving about their business, a small group sitting cross-legged, facing the early sun. Both Walden and New Dawn came walking towards us, the kelpie beside them. Walden had his hair tied back in a ponytail, just like Gina sometimes did, though his hair wasn't all black and shiny. It felt a bit odd seeing a man with a ponytail, but I knew he was a good person so I didn't think about it anymore.

New Dawn's eyes were red and she didn't hide the reason: "Love this dog. Right from the start, she just had this aura. A bit of me hopes you're wrong, but knowing Snarkey I wouldn't put it past him. But if you're right, then... then she has a path to follow. It's like it's meant to be. She finds a loving home; gets stolen by some...well, you know; gets rescued; gets adopted; returns to loving home. It's a circle, boys, a beautiful circle." With that New Dawn turned and walked away.

"It's okay, boys. New Dawn doesn't know it, but before the day has seen its course she will be holding a nine week old red kelpie puppy, a boy. And this will become his right place, where he belongs."

At the start the kelpie walked beside us, next to Whippet, but the closer we got to Mrs M's the more she would rush ahead, before returning. As we neared Mrs M's street, there was no stopping her. She started up this howling sound, loud and persistent. By the time we reached the house the howling was the loudest I'd heard any dog make. She was hurling herself at the front door and when it swung open she launched herself into Mrs M's arms. You would have thought it would have taken Mrs M by surprise, knocked her side-ways, but she caught the dog in her arms as if they were both part of some seamless circus performance. Mrs M gave a loud shriek of happiness. "Thought I'd lost you, thought I'd lost you too." Lisatoa and I stood a moment and saw cuddling and snuggling that told us this was the completion of "a beautiful circle". We would be sure to tell New Dawn.

Mrs M and the kelpie then disappeared down the hallway, not even a glance back at us. But the door was left wide open and in we went. By the time we reached the kitchen, Mrs M was seated in one chair and the kelpie in one right beside her. She had her arm around her dog. The kelpie looked settled and very happy as if she had never been away. "Let's shake on our reunion," Mrs M said, "let's shake." The dog put out her right front leg and shook hands with Mrs M. "Well done Clever, well done. I reckon you re-member all your tricks. Well done, Clever."

"That's her name? Is that her name?" I asked, "You called her Clever?"

"That'd be the truth of it. I know, not much of a dog's name. Just called her Dog at first."

"But her name is Clever?"

"Yes, indeed. Smartest dog I ever saw. So, the name Clever fits like a glove." It was most definitely the completion of "a beautiful circle."

We told Mrs M Clever's story and at the part about Snarkey she said some colourful and descriptive words, all of which we agreed with. She told us how she had "a right blue" with Snarkey and had refused to pay a ridiculous bill when the problem hadn't been properly fixed. When we told her about the hippies and the com-mune, Mrs M said, "Well, well. They sound good people. Wouldn't have thought that. Changes my opinion." Mrs M then waved her arm and said, "Oh, where's my manners? Take a seat, gentlemen."

For a short time, I'd almost forgotten about the diaries which lay on top of the table, most of them open. Pieces of paper mark-ing particular pages stuck out of the diaries and a notepad lay beside them, full of messy writing. It looked like a kitchen table that had seen a lot of reading, writing and thinking.

I looked at the diaries and at Mrs M's dog and thought how Randolph and Clever were both home now.

"I've made a pie, boys, an apple pie, with a choko or two added," Mrs M said as she went over to the bench. It was very quiet in the kitchen at that moment, only the sound of a knife cutting pastry and the scraping of plates. When Mrs M turned around her eyes were very wet, ready to spill tears.

"Let me get those," Lisatoa said, and he took the plates off her and put them on the table. He then turned back to Mrs M and put his arm through hers and led her to a chair and helped her sit. When she was seated, he stood there patting her back. Lisatoa was well on the way to developing a thoughtful, kindness streak. But I already knew that.

"Thank you for the diaries lads. Young men. There are bits that made me happy, lots that made me sad. Mostly sad. No mum would want to lose her son, it's all the wrong way around, not how it should be. I don't expect you to understand that. Well, not completely." I remembered that time when I was leaving to go to Lisatoa's dad's birthday and I heard my mum say, "I can't stop loving you" and it made me think that I just might understand such things. Then I thought of the diaries and my postcards, especially my postcards, and I knew for certain that I did understand such things.

"But more importantly," Mrs M continued, "there's things in here that Alex needs to know. Won't fix everything up for Alex. Can't bring a dad back. But it might explain things. Maybe not now, but later. He needs to understand and if he can do that perhaps some of his crazy stuff will go away, he might lose some of his rage. Needs to know he was loved. Yeah, that first. Love first, then the rest will follow." I might be becoming the writer, but I still think that last sentence of Mrs M's sounded pretty good.

146

It was quiet in the kitchen for a while, until I asked, "What happened to his mum, Alex's mum?"

"Ha, who knows? She shot through. It's why I live here, why I've got Alex. Had Alex. Randolph had been in the army about a year and she shoots through with some bloke. Less said about that the better. She told Alex it was all because of the army, made Alex believe her. It's why he burnt those uniforms, Scouts' uniforms. Why he hates the bush, jungle he calls it. No excuses, I know, but it explains. Train off its tracks doesn't know where it's going, what it's doing." Mrs M's last sentence was also a pretty good one.

"Is Alex still at the special school?" Lisatoa asked.

"Special school? Ha! That what you call it? Yes, he's still at that place."

"The diaries, so, are you going to give him the diaries?" I asked.

"Most certainly. Not all of them, not all of them. At least not for a bit anyway. Later on they will all be his. Bit at the time though." Mrs M paused a moment, then continued. "Maybe, later on, way in the future, you could take him to the cave? No rush, but later on. What do you think?" We both nodded and meant it because all those things that Alex had done no longer made us angry. That Harper Lee sure knew a thing or two.

"Eat up, boys," she said. I'm sure the apple and choko pie was delicious, but we didn't really taste it.

It was a couple of weeks later when we saw Alex. It was after school and Lisatoa and I were in Keane's Groceries, where Mr Keane had installed this ice machine. You paid Mr Keane and he gave you a paper cup and plastic spoon which you then took over to the shiny new machine that looked like it could have come out of some spaceship. You then pressed this button and finely crushed iced poured into your cup. Sometimes the flow of ice wouldn't stop, spilling over the floor until Mr Keane had to leave whoever he was serving and rush over to stop it. He would then give us a brush and pan to sweep up the spilled ice, which always seemed to melt quicker than we could brush and pan it. Other times no crushed ice came out, but Mr Keane didn't rush over at those times. When you got your cup of crushed ice you could choose a bright red or green syrup to pour over the ice. You then got to eat the ice, but had to do it slowly in order to avoid that brain freeze thing. It tasted pretty good, just the thing for after school. I liked drinking the melting ice and syrup, even if I then ended up with a lump of plain ice. It was pointless asking Mr Keane for some more syrup. One day, when Lisatoa wasn't with me, I bought Gina a red crushed ice. It was a bit awkward when I gave it to her, she looked as if she thought it was some sort of trick and waited a few moments before she took it. I left her with it and pretended to be looking at some very interesting groceries. She never thanked me, but I'm still glad I gave it to her because it made her lips a glossy shiny red. I was also glad that Stephan was there and saw me giving Gina the red crushed ice. Mr Keane soon got rid of the ice machine, which I think was a pity. He said it "wasn't worth the effort, too messy, no money in it, just not good for anything really." I should have told him to "consider things from *my* point of view... climb inside *my* skin and walk around in it." Then the ice machine would have been around for years and years.

So, it was one of those times when Lisatoa and I were leaving Keane's Groceries with our crushed ices that we saw Alex. He was across the street, sitting on one of the bus seats, all hunched up, arms crossed as if he was cold. It didn't seem as if he was happy at that moment, but when he looked up and saw Lisatoa and me he smiled and gave us a little wave, which I thought was pretty good. If he'd then asked us to take him to the cave we would have. But he didn't ask, which I think was smart because some things shouldn't be rushed.

I wanted to show this last section to my mum, but couldn't work out whether it would make her happy to read about the whole MacGregor family or really sad, so I decided it would be best to ask Lisatoa's mum again.

For the next bit of my writing I needed to start using my third HB pencil. I still had the last bits of the first two, couldn't throw them away after their good service, but they had gotten too short to comfortably hold; emergency use only from now on. So, number three was needed. I decided I would try not to press as heavily and to sharpen more carefully, so that number three would last.

JUST KEEP SINGING

One of my favourite places was the second-storey verandah at the front of Lisatoa's house. We just liked sitting there, peering through the camphorwood tree down to the river. It was a huge camphorwood tree, maybe sixty or seventy feet high and its trunk was so big that even Lisatoa's dad couldn't put his arms around it. There were lots of these trees along the river, but our one was the biggest. Last summer the council wanted to get rid of these trees, said they were an invasive species, but they never got around to it, and I'm glad they didn't because I like those trees. I know they're not supposed to be here (they're from Asia somewhere), but like Lisatoa's mum said, "Neither are we when it comes to it." The camphorwood tree is a bit like the lantana bushes that you can see in lots of places where they slowly choke the bush, but they've got these beautiful little flowers, a kaleidoscope of colours. And they smell nice. I've also got a soft spot for foxes. Yeah, I know what they do to our wildlife, which includes our possums. But if you stumbled upon a fox some early morning and he held your eyes with a knowing stare, even for the briefest of moments, to then glide away all sleek and silent into the growing light, you might then think something different about them. It's all a bit confusing I suppose, all a bit hard to reconcile. Sounds like a job for a philosopher.

One time when we were sitting on the verandah, Lisatoa decided to jump across to one of the lower branches of the camphorwood. He then climbed way up, not all the way because that would be almost as crazy as jumping into a flooding river to save what you thought was a wallaby. Lisatoa then sat on one of the branches, leant against the trunk and pretended to be asleep. I could never jump across to that branch and I could most definitely not climb up that high, but when Lisatoa was pretending to be asleep I closed my eyes and tried, really tried, to imagine what it must be like. And after a bit I thought I knew how the camphorwood leaves were rustling in the breeze, how they felt between my fingers and the rich camphor smell they gave off. I could look into the small white flowers and see their intricate detail, I could feel the roughness of the bark against my back, see flickering sunlight dappling my hand. So, I could never climb that camphorwood tree. At least not like Lisatoa could. I think that has to be the first memorable example of my muse and imagination hitting it off together, and that's why I told you about it at the beginning of this chapter.

If you were sitting on that verandah and looked off to the side you would see the mountain range that slides all the way along the western horizon. Sometimes I thought it looked like one of those cartoons of a snake, its back arching and dipping along. The mountains are a lush and deep green, clear and sharp in the morning sun. By afternoon they seem a little faded as if the long hot day has drained them. Afternoon storms are best, those summer storms when you can feel the heat building as if it's a pressure that must eventually burst. On those afternoons the mountains get this bruised blue colour and the tops get wreathed in swirling white mists that look like some fantasy from which something good and magical might come, or something dark and evil.

It was the holiday before our last term in primary school. We had been on that verandah for most of the afternoon listening to records on an old record player Lisatoa had secretly borrowed from his sisters. We lay on our backs on the wooden slats of the verandah and each time a record finished I'd turn on my side to watch the arm of the player lift and move away to let the next record flop down, to then return and lower itself onto the black vinyl. It's not good if a record gets left in the sun because it will warp. But if you are lying on your side and a warped record is playing it can be very soothing and hypnotic to watch the record arm undulate like a canoe riding some friendly swell. Whenever the Beatles or Gerry and the Pacemakers came on, or any other group we liked, I'd find myself humming along and sometimes singing if I knew the words. I must've sounded awful, could never hold a tune, any tune, but in my mind I thought I was sounding quite wonderful. We had cheese and lettuce sandwiches for lunch. Those sandwiches might sound plain and ordinary, but I remember them tasting delicious, the bread softer, lettuce crunchier, cheese cheesier than ever before. You just don't get many afternoons that good.

It must have been around four o'clock, we were still lounging around on the verandah when there was a sudden burst of wind that rattled and shook the leaves of the camphorwood. The air smelt different then, it had a presence, a weight and pressure to it, electric and promising change. We looked towards the west and there were those misty clouds writhing over the arched snake-back of the mountains. Heavy dark clouds sat above them, roiling down the escarpment and hinterland, churning towards us. "Ah, it's the Storm God," Lisatoa said, "and he's coming for us."

I knew I needed to head home before the rain came, but was slow to move as if waking from some deep sleep that still clung to the last lovely remnants of dreams. The sky had already darkened when I was leaving and the rain had started, at first falling in cold heavy splats. A loud clap of thunder drowned out whatever Lisatoa's parting words were and he had to repeat them, yelling them at me as I moved into the storm. "Keep singing," he said, "you must keep singing!" I thought he was making fun of me.

The rain, strangely cold for such a storm, began to fall heavily as I ran home and by the time I arrived I was saturated and shivering. Mum tossed me some towels before I was allowed into the house. "You'll catch yourself a death," she told me, "out in all that water, you'll catch yourself a death."

"No way," I told her, "it's just some rain. Besides, Miss says a bit of cold, like the rain, can't give you a cold."

In the morning I woke with a runny nose and a bit of a headache. So much for Miss' medical knowledge. It had rained heavily all night and when I looked out the window the sky was a dark grey, the rain sheeting down, more a curtain of water than falling rain. The local radio, which mum had on each morning, spoke of flash-flooding in town, "with the worst yet to come, given the record breaking falls in the mountains and hinterland. Get your arks ready folks, might be the time for some miracles." The radio man then laughed because he thought he'd been witty and funny and because it was what he did every morning.

I'd planned to go back to Lisatoa's, but the rain wouldn't let up. I wanted to lie on that verandah again and listen to more music, capture that afternoon again. Instead I spent the day in my loungeroom chair reading some more of *To Kill a Mockingbird*, with the rain a constant drumming on our roof. Occasionally, there'd be a wind squall and rain would lash against our window, giving an almost underwater view of all outside until the water's slow slide down.

After dinner, where I ate too many samosas, could never help myself, mum and I went into the loungeroom. We settled into our chairs, cocooned once more in our reading lamps' domes of light. I was getting close to the end of *To Kill a Mockingbird* and it's just the sort of book you can't keep away from, especially in those closing pages. No wonder Randolph liked it. It just might be the first book I would read more than once. Mum leant over in her chair and switched on the radio. The volume was low, but I could still hear The Lovin' Spoonful singing "Daydream". I sure liked that song, but tried not to listen, because I was finishing a book; I didn't want to be just reading the words, I wanted to be *in* the book, moving around where it's set, with the characters right beside me, or even closer. Just for a while I wanted to be that character called Scout. Then mum kept turning the dial until she found one of those classical stations, the music all smooth and soft, and that was just fine.

Maybe it was the classical music, but I didn't get to finish *To Kill a Mockingbird* that night because I fell asleep. Didn't even make it to bed, just drifted off in my chair. In fact, it must have been the music because when I stirred one time and lifted an eyelid I saw mum fast asleep in her chair. I knew I should go to bed, but it was so nice in the chair, the bed could wait a bit longer.

At first I ignored the loud banging. Still half asleep, caught between worlds, I thought it must be the thunder, or one of the loose pieces of our corrugated iron roof flapping in the storm. I was having a warm and delicious sleep, so I rolled around a little in my chair and tried to delve back into that comfortable space. But the banging continued, then I sneezed twice and needed to find my hanky for a runny nose. Nobody's ever happy to catch a cold, but that one time I was. I listened to the banging and the ongoing heavy rain, but there was another noise, a noise sometimes buried in the other sounds, sometimes coming out on top. In that half-sleep I thought that other noise was like a drowning person being pulled under, but pushing to the surface again, arm waving, refusing to give up, wanting to be grabbed and taken in. And I just knew that it was me who had to find out about that noise, I was supposed to grab that arm.

I wasn't certain where that other noise was coming from, the one weaving in and out of the banging and the storm, but I made my way towards the front of our house, and as I moved the sound grew clearer. It was a screeching sound, a high-pitched wailing. Through the small, frosted glass panels of our front door I could see two shapes thrashing around like flimsy branches in a lashing wind. As I moved towards the door, I felt my mother coming up beside me and as I turned to look at her there was the sound of shattering glass and suddenly the hallway was full of the sounds of storm and madness. A face appeared at the broken window, then a second face behind it. I knew them, hair plastered to their heads, faces screwed up and distorted, eyes red-rimmed, but I knew them straight away: Lisatoa's sisters. The moment I opened the door, Moana, cut hand bleeding, reached out and grabbed my left arm at the very end and began tugging on it as if it was just a normal arm.

"You've got to come, got to come. Now. Now!" Moana yelled as she stood in the doorway, water running down her body and onto the floor. She continued screaming, waving her arms around, then grabbed my left arm again and started to drag me outside.

"Do... do your parents... what's going on? Oh dear, you're cut..." Whatever else my mum was saying became lost in the wind and rain.

"You've got to come. You have to come. It's Lisatoa, it's Lisatoa. It's Lisatoa. He's in hospital. The canoe. You've got to come," Moana screamed.

Then I was running through the falling rain with Lisatoa's sisters. For a short moment I could still hear mum calling out to me, but I had no idea what she was saying; not that it would have mattered, because I was running barefoot through the rain, heading towards where I had to be. Water, ankle deep, flowed along the road, churning and gurgling along the gutters, foaming and circling down drains. Streetlights were muted by the falling rain. I kicked something, knew I'd cut my big toe, trod on loose gravel that dug into the soles of my feet, but it would have taken a lot more to stop me. We were speeding past Mr Vincenti's fruit shop, past the darkened windows of Dr Petroni's surgery, closed early that night, when Linda went sprawling forward, her face and hands crashing through the water and on to the concrete of the footpath. When she pushed herself up we could see in the light that spilled from Keane's Groceries that the side of her face and the palms of her hands were bleeding. I looked down at my toe and knew immediately that that wasn't a good idea. My toenail had been torn off and it looked bloody and messy. If I hadn't been heading to Lisatoa, if I'd been in the backyard at home, I would have had a quick look, then started screaming and crying, refusing to ever take another look because that just makes it all the worse. But when I was outside Keane's Grocery and looked down at my toe, I felt nothing more than the need to keep moving. I knew Tobias and his mum would have kept going. I bet Percy Fawcett wouldn't have stopped to have a cry. And I reckon Alex's dad would have pushed on. And... and my dad too. Later I thought I must have gotten a bit of each of those characters in me, just a little bit, but just enough. I didn't need to know the details of what had happened to Lisatoa; that he was in hospital was more than enough.

We struggled on through the storm and if anyone had stumbled upon us they would have seen three bedraggled people looking manic, and bleeding. We came to the beginning of the driveway that leads to the hospital, about half a mile long with mown edges and an avenue of overhanging coral trees. Some of the lights that lined the driveway had gone out, while others flickered eerily as if deciding whether to tip over into the darkness. Squalls of wind whipped the branches of the trees, leaves flying to escape, some blood red flowers still clinging on in the wavering lights.

We slowed our pace as we moved down the middle of the driveway, letting some calm and energy return for whatever lay ahead. When we got to a curve in the driveway we could see that one of the coral trees had blown over, its roots pointing skywards like arms held high in surrender. The tree blocked the driveway, but we were able to climb through the branches, careful to try and avoid the thorns. We were close, just a little further.

ROOM 21

Then the hospital was in front of us, an old one-storey red-brick building, constantly being repaired and patched, like some patient who would never be completely fine. The grey tile roof was slick with running water, gutters overflowing like waterfalls trying to hide what lay behind. We moved towards the entrance, rain thundering on the corrugated roof of the front awning. When we stepped forward the automatic doors juddered open and a reception area of plastic chairs and fluorescent lighting lay before us. It was a cold room where sad and worried people had waited and hoped, waited and hoped. Moana again took hold of my left arm and led me down a long corridor, past rooms of sleeping patients and whispering nurses.

Room 21 was a room of shadows, grey ghosts stooping to look down on a bed that tilted upwards so that Lisatoa was half sitting, half lying down, as if suspended between two choices. His head was heavily bandaged, one eye hidden behind white bandages, the other closed. He looked little. A few strands of his light red hair stuck out, flattened against his forehead. There was a smile on his face like he was gently sleeping, immersed in pleasant dreams. Moana and Linda moved straight into the room to nestle between their parents. Dr Petroni stood at the other side of the bed reading whatever information the glow and beep of strange machines was putting out. I stood on the threshold of room 21 unable to go any further, as if the closer I got the worse things would turn out to be. I didn't know what had happened, but you don't need to be too smart to know that this was bad, very bad. I had the urge to turn around and run, climb the fallen coral tree, then sprint like never before, trying to outrun whatever was in room 21.

Linda stopped looking at Lisatoa and turned to beckon me into the room. When I didn't move, she came over and took my arm, my left arm again, and tried to lead me into the room. But I couldn't budge, just couldn't, legs frozen. She then leant towards me and said, "Lisatoa wants you to come and see him." It was then that someone must have made my legs move, because there I was beside the bed where I stood staring, wanting answers to a thousand questions I couldn't ask. In a darkened corner of the room I saw the statue that had always been in Iosepha's workshop. It must have been almost impossible to get it there, but if anyone could do that it would have been Lisatoa's dad. That statue had a lot of watching over and protecting to do and when I looked more closely its face was still wet from the rain, looking as if it had been crying; but it was still a face that looked stern and determined to play its part. I then heard a movement from under the bed and looking down saw Whippet lying there. Her head was resting beside her front paw, and it gave me the feeling that things were getting into place, like it was just as essential that the statue and Whippet be there as any of the medical machines.

"We don't have the necessary equipment," Dr Petroni said, "and even if we did, we don't have the expertise. I'm an ordinary general practitioner and this is a small country hospital. It is good here, but it's not enough. I've done what I can, he's stable now, but the brain is tricky. Sydney, he's going to Sydney tomorrow. They have neurologists, they have the equipment. It's arranged. I'd send him now if I could, but this storm..." Dr Petroni's words trailed into silence. He raised both hands, palms upwards and slowly shook his head. "Tomorrow, we'll see tomorrow. I will stay here all night. I won't sleep." I thought he sounded a little sad and I wanted to tell him that whatever an ordinary general practitioner might be, he wasn't one of them.

Dr Petroni then turned to quietly leave the room. As he passed me, he put his hand on the top of my head and whispered how he would call my home, let mum know what was going on. And it must have been his placing his hand on the top of my head that did it, his hand must have punctured all that pressure that had built up inside me. I began to cry, not a silent trickling of a tear or two, but a sobbing that was coming from somewhere deep inside me. I knew it wasn't a good thing to be doing, it wasn't about me and getting anyone's attention. But I couldn't stop, and when I tried to stall it, even for a moment, it came back even worse. My face was a mess, my cheeks smeared with tears I tried to wipe away, my lips and chin covered in the mucus that ran from my nose. I knew it wasn't pretty, but it wouldn't stop, something was making it happen, something, not me. Listatoa's dad turned and walked slowly towards me, and maybe it was the lighting, or maybe my blurred vision, but he looked bigger than I had ever seen him, even bigger than that time on the jetty when he pulled Lisatoa out of the river. I thought he might be going to tell me to get out, go away, we do not need this now. But he didn't. He bent forward and kissed me on the forehead and once on each cheek. He then took hold of the end of my left arm, gently squeezing it, and leant across to my right ear and said, "We can do this. You and me." Then he was back beside Lisatoa's bed and I was no longer crying. Somehow a small handtowel found its way into my right hand and I used it to wipe my face, before moving to where I knew I should be.

Whispering, they told me what had happened, each person weaving in their part of the story, each holding on to their connection to Lisatoa. I took in what they were saying, seeing it all as if present. Lisatoa had been reckless. No, that's too kind, that's avoiding the truth. He'd been stupid. Really, really stupid. He talked about gods, but he wasn't one and he should have known that. Stupid. And inconsiderate, I should add, and not just because of me, but because when Lisatoa gets hurt he hurts lots of those around him. That's how it works with friends and family;

there's a bond and you try not to do anything that breaks it. I know that now.

Who the heck gets in a canoe in the sort of weather we were experiencing? Worst storm in decades they were saying on the radio, been raging nearly twenty-four hours, a cyclone the commentator said. "Stay indoors if you can folks, not even weather for ducks." So, who gets in a canoe in that sort of weather? Lisatoa? Correct. Moana, Linda and Whippet were with him when he went out to make sure the canoes were above the level of the flooding river. He'd dragged the first one further up, away from the churning brown of the river. Started to drag the second one when he saw a raft spinning and bucking in the centre of the river, caught in some whirlpool. It was one of those inflatable rubber ones, the sort kids might play in in the shallows of the beach or estuary. They couldn't see anyone in it, tippy toe on the jetty they still couldn't see anyone in it. But Lisatoa just had to check, he said some little kid, a baby even, could be unconscious and lying down, so he just had to check.

"We tried to stop him," Linda said, "we really tried, but he wouldn't listen. Just ignored me. Like always." She paused, her hand touching the side of her face, a distracted exploring of the new terrain of cuts and scrapes. "He wouldn't listen to what we said, even when we yelled," Linda continued. "Tried grabbing his arms, but he just shrugged us off. 'I'll be fine,' he said. But when Whippet jumped into the canoe beside him he lifted her out and back onto the jetty. So, what does that tell you, eh? Eh?"

"I kept yelling at him," Moana said, "then I sent Linda to get mum and dad. I told him, "You're going to be in so much trouble, so much trouble when dad gets hold of you." Then I tried something else. This usually works. Sometimes. I said to him all sooky and soft, "Please don't go. We don't want you to do this." Perhaps he didn't hear me, but he must have heard the howling Whippet started up, an angry and fierce howling that went right through the sounds of river and storm. But even Whippet couldn't stop him."

Moana then told me how at the same time Lisatoa pushed the canoe out their dad came thundering out of the house, their mother following, and he had a look on his face that said he was not to be messed with, a look that said punishment will be swift and severe, and ongoing. "I was scared," Moana said, "I was scared and it wasn't even me doing something stupid and naughty. It was something he definitely, most definitely, knew he shouldn't be doing, not after his rescuing Whippet. Dad grabbed the other canoe and carried it into the swirling water. His left leg, knee height, was hit by a large branch, but he pushed it aside as if it were a small twig. Dad ran deeper into the river pushing the canoe beside him until he launched it forward and jumped into it."

"He was lucky it didn't sink, lucky it didn't sink, lucky," Linda told me, speaking far too quickly as if her words were out of control. "It was pretty close, but he didn't sink it. Lucky though. It didn't sink. He looked really funny in it. Like a big man trying to ride a tricycle. Pretty funny, eh?" She then gave out a hollow and high-pitched laugh that made her sound a bit crazy and only stopped when her mum put her arms around her.

"When Lisatoa reached the rubber raft it broke free of the whirlpool and began to rush off, as if running away from him. It was then that he stood up in his canoe," Moana said. "How dumb. He stood up because I reckon he wanted to look inside the stupid runaway raft. He turned to us, grinned his stupid boofhead grin, and yelled out, "It's empty, no baby. It's completely..." He didn't finish that sentence. He didn't finish it because... You don't stand up in a canoe, do you? Do you?" Moana looked at us, but we didn't need to give an answer.

"His canoe bucked, like a rodeo horse wanting him off its back," Lisatoa's dad said, "and he was thrown back. I will always remember his arms waving like crazy, flapping, trying to fly back to standing up. He was thrown back and his head hit the back of the canoe."

"It was like a crack of thunder, a crack of thunder. I heard it. In all that storm I heard it. It was deeper than proper thunder. Worse, just worse," Lisatoa's mum said.

"Don't know what would have happened if he'd fallen into the river, just don't know. Small mercies, small mercies," Lisatoa's dad said, shaking his head. "Got him ashore. Then rushed here."

Just then Dr Petroni returned. "Checked the x-rays again. No fractured skull. No, no... before you say anything, it doesn't mean everything is okay. Could be bruising and, I don't want to alarm you, but best you know, could be bruising and bleeding. Of the brain. That's why I've arranged for Sydney. In the meantime it would be a good sign if Lisatoa were to regain consciousness. A very good sign."

The room fell silent when Dr Petroni left, the only noise the storm outside and a dripping sound which I thought must have been coming from one of the machines. The dripping sound became a little faster, louder and more rhythmic. In the seriousness and silence of the room it was a sound that caught your attention, until it seemed to want to crowd out all other thoughts. Just the dripping, dripping, dripping. Almost mesmerising, until from the corner of the room there was a brief slithering sound. Then silence again until the dripping sound returned, at first irregular, then rhythmic once more. It wasn't just me drawn to the sound; Moana and Linda started towards the corner of the room.

"Rain's coming in," Linda said, "it's coming through the wall."

Lisatoa's mum flicked on the overhead fluorescent light, a cold and antiseptic light, a hospital light. We could see that water had seeped into the corner of the room, dripping from the cornice. The faded brown of a water stain and some peeling paint said how the roof had leaked before. Again, there was the slithering of built up water, snaking down to a growing circle of damp carpet. This time the dripping didn't start up again, but the corner of the wall seemed to be moving, bulging, as if something was in there, wanting out. The skin of the paint was being pushed out by the build-up of water; it was like a balloon, bulging, bulging, growing bigger and bigger as it grew down the wall. Then it burst and water gushed down the side of the wall. A piece of the cornice came away, allowing more water to flow in. Just like a small river.

"It's like a little river," I said.

Lisatoa's dad quickly turned as if I'd said something completely inappropriate or incredibly stupid. He stared at me and I thought his eyes were like hooks that had dug into me, drawing me in. "Now is the time. Now, Ray!" I had no idea what he meant, but knew that whatever it was, I would do it. He moved over to me and took hold of the end of my arm, wrapping it in his huge hand. It felt as if all his fingers were pulsing, massaging the end of my arm. "Now, it must be now," he said. "We must sing him back. Like before. The river again. It has come to us. We did it before. On the jetty. Again, we will do it again. Tie him with sound, sing him back out of the darkness." When he took his hand away my left arm felt strange; it felt weird, but it also felt nice. I'd had that same feeling before, that time on the jetty, like my hand was there, a whole arm, and it felt strong. I knew it couldn't be there, not really, but it felt like it was there, and it felt right and good. And ready.

"Put the lights out," Lisatoa's dad ordered, "put the overhead lights out." Without any questions Lisatoa's mum moved to the light switch on the wall beside the door. Fluorescent light from the hallway still spilled into the room, and I moved to quickly close the door. I knew what was going on, but if you'd asked me to explain I couldn't have told you. But I still knew. Moana leaned over and put out the small light above Lisatoa's bed, and I wondered if she too knew exactly what was happening. Maybe they all understood what was going on. Some small lights, red, blue and white still flickered from the machines beside the bed, but I thought they were just fine; they looked like the few remaining stars just before dawn, twinkling new day promises.

It might have been dark in room 21, but I knew exactly where everyone was, as if all arranged. I could still hear the storm outside, along with the flow of water, the little river sliding down the wall. If anything, it was getting louder, as if wanting to take over the room. Then it was Lisatoa's dad's voice that began to dominate all the other sounds. It started out as a low but insistent humming that seemed to want to gently usher away all other sounds. It was like the sounds he had been making that time on the jetty, but then something else started to come into it. At first it was a background sound, an irregular beat, a guttural huff, that punctuated the humming, but it grew more regular and equal to the volume of his humming. Then I knew what the sound was, it was like the sound of a heart beating, pulsing, getting stronger. I heard Moana join in the humming, melodic and cajoling. Linda followed, at first sounding tentative and frightened, but growing into a sound that seemed full of pleading. From the other side of Lisatoa's bed came his mother's voice, strong and clear, a humming that seemed an order, an imperative. I couldn't hear the storm anymore, or the water running into the room, just four different voices making one song, weaving all through the room, crossing over each other, coming together and moving apart as if they were different strands wanting to entwine into a single rope.

"Ray!" Lisatoa's dad called, a voice sounding more like a yelp or bark. It took me by surprise, made me jump a little, but that one word, heavily encoded, told me what I should be doing, what I should have been doing right from the beginning; I wasn't spectator here, I was participant. I started my humming, had to clear my throat and start again. But it didn't sound right, my voice didn't seem to fit in. It was like my tinny little effort could ruin things, disrupt the weaving sound of those perfect voices. It had sounded fine before, down at the jetty when there was just me and Lisatoa's dad singing, but not now, not this time. I would be the weak spot, the frayed flaw in the rope, and then this thing, this binding, would snap.

I stopped my humming, and when I did I knew exactly what I had to do. I'd done it a little bit that time at the jetty, even though I felt stupid doing it. I was to put both my arms out, they were to go in front of me and they were to search the darkness to find the four voices, find the four strands and take hold of them. When I put my arms out I knew I would need two hands, and I also knew that when I needed them they would be there, they would be there. I stretched my arms out, and my right hand started curling at the fingers, beckoning things closer. But the voices remained disparate, adrift from each other; there was harmony, but it was of four strands, none strong enough on their own to do what was needed. The four had to be one, then there might just be enough for what was needed.

I kept beckoning with my right hand, but became aware that something was happening on the end of my left arm, a tingling turning to an ache, finishing in an agony as if the end of my arm had been shoved into hot coals. I felt that if I lowered that left arm then the pain would cease. But so would everything else. I kept my left arm out and clenched my eyes shut as if further blindness in the darkened room would make it harder for the pain to seek me out. I felt tears run down my cheek, but I was not going to put my left arm down.

"No, I won't," I called out. "No." I had called loud enough to go above the sound of those voices, loud enough to be clearly heard, but no one responded. "No," I called out again. The pain in my left arm seemed to slide away, a slow retreating, and in its place I had a hand, it felt as if there was a hand on the end of my left arm. At first it felt rigid; it was there, but I couldn't give it movement, couldn't put life into it. A wave of four voices washed over me, washed through me, and the hand began to move, fingers slowly loosening. Both arms were stretched, two hands beckoning, drawing the ends of four voices closer and closer, until it was as if I held four strands in my two hands. The four voices ceased being separate and became one, impossible to identify any single voice as they wove in and out of each other, plaiting a single rope of strength.

Now it was up to me to see it through to completion. Things, forces, were being held in place by the others in the room, things were being done, but such effort couldn't last. There was a moment, a brief window, and it had to be taken. I imagined the rope winding hold of Lisatoa, finding him in the dark, winding him tight and close, and dragging him back. I clasped my hands together, holding the rope and pulling as hard as I could and slowly walking backwards. I could feel sweat under my arms and across my forehead.

Then I was falling, tripping over one of the chairs that had been behind me. I cried out as I went over the chair, knocking it sideways, to come crashing down onto the floor. The noise killed the four voices. I tried to break my fall, splaying two hands out behind me, but it didn't work, it didn't work, couldn't work. There was silence in room 21 until I heard the door opening and the click of the light switch as the room again filled with the flash of cold fluorescent light.

"What happened?" Dr Petroni was standing in the doorway. "What's going on?"

"I don't know. I fell over," I told him. And that was as close as I ever got to explaining what had gone on in room 21.

As I sat there on the floor, I looked at my left arm. It was as it had always been, there was no left hand. Maybe I should have been flooded with a sadness or a disappointment, like waking from a beautiful dream and finding out that was all it was, but I was too eager to get close to Lisatoa. I got up from the floor, but Lisatoa's parents and sisters blocked my view. I edged in between Moana and Linda and when I looked at Lisatoa I suddenly felt empty inside, as if everything had dropped out. Nothing had changed, he still lay there unmoving, unconscious. No magic had been worked. And I knew it had been my fault; there had been the voices, the strands and then the rope, they had done their part, they had made a lifeline and all I had to do was use it. But the final action had not been completed.

A nurse appeared in the doorway, and with her was my mum. "Let's take you home, eh? Parked just down the driveway, other side of some fallen tree." I didn't want to go home, but I couldn't stay in room 21, couldn't look in the eyes of any of the people I'd let down, just couldn't. Walking out of the room, I took a last look at the statue, the rain had dried and it no longer looked as if it was crying, it looked to be glowing soft and warm. Just a statue, I thought, just a stupid statue. Before we left, Dr Petroni cleaned up the toe I had kicked and throughout it all I felt nothing; he could just as well have been working on my left hand.

It seemed to take me an age to get ready for bed. Sometimes, I'd pause, confused as to what I was doing. My bandaged toe was stained with blood. I dug through my drawers, dropping clothes everywhere. When I found them they smelt musty and coarse to the touch. My old lucky pyjamas from years and years ago, pyjamas covered with pictures of Winnie the Pooh, Christopher Robin, Piglet, Eeyore, all old friends from a time and place where nothing bad could stay. I put them on, faded and ill-fitting, but I just needed to be wrapped in that sort of comfort.

I got into bed that night, thinking there was no way I would be able to fall asleep. But one moment I was reliving what had happened in room 21, the incessant rain as background, when I must have fallen asleep. Around four, or even five, can't really be sure, I snarled my bandaged toe in the sheets and it hurt to turn over. I lay there in the rumpled sheets, tormented between sleep and wakefulness, thinking of Lisatoa trapped in the cold and stiff whiteness of his hospital bed. I drifted back towards sleep, and in restless dreams I saw Lisatoa's white sheets cover him like some dead body. There was no movement, no rise and fall of breathing, just the motionless outline of his body. I leaned forward, and it might have been my left hand, a cruel tease, that reached out, grabbed the sheet and pulled it away like some magician revealing his trick. But there was no magic. When I pulled the sheet away there was nothing there and I turned to Lisatoa's crying family, grinned and said, "Ta-da!" Again and again I replaced the sheet over Lisatoa's bed and again and again I pulled it back, always ending with the stupid grin and the "Ta-da!" And in that fitful nightmare I knew I would keep pulling back the sheet until Lisatoa was there, wide awake and well.

When I woke it was with a jolt, my heart pounding, my body sticky with sweat. Running through my mind was the same question over and over: "What had I done? What had I done?" The rain had stopped, no drumming on the roof, no gurgling gutters. I stumbled to my window to peer out and the sky was clear, apart from the few remaining stars just before dawn, twinkling new day promises.

I took off my Winnie the Pooh pyjamas, scrunched them up and threw them into the corner of my room, and got dressed.

The phone was ringing, sounding distant and lonely. No one answered and whoever had called would stay distant and lost. The ringing started up again and I could hear mum's muffled voice. When I got into the kitchen she was putting the receiver back. "That was Dorothea, your teacher, Miss Windsor. She'd heard the news, wanted to know if I knew anything new. Told her about Sydney, but that's about it." The phone started up again and this time it was Clarry. Another call and it was Mrs M. Yet another call and this time mum's hand flew to her throat and she took a step back as if frightened by the words she'd heard. She held the phone towards me, holding the receiver by the cord so that it dangled like something being hanged.

"Some news for you, young man," Dr Petroni said, "but it looks like someone else is demanding to give it to you."

Then it was Moana on the phone and her words, no break between them, ran fast and clear like one of the streams in the mountains. Lisatoa had woken up and apart from a sore head seemed to be his normal self and wanted to know about breakfast. She lowered her voice and slowly said, "We did it, you know. We did it." As I hung up the phone, there was a knocking at the door and when I opened it Walden and New Dawn were there. As soon as I saw Walden I threw my arm around him, laughing out aloud as the small kelpie New Dawn held in her arms yapped and yelped, spreading the good news.

I would go and visit Lisatoa in the hospital, but before that I had to go back to my bedroom, pick up my Winnie the Pooh pyjamas, smooth them out, fold them and neatly place them away in their new spot, top drawer right beside my postcards.

I wasn't sure who I should show this section of my writing to, or even if I should show it to anyone at all. In the end, I showed it to Gina, which I can tell you was a surprise even to myself. I told myself I gave it to her because she was smarter than me; which was true. I told myself I gave it to her because she could be all objective and critical; which was true. I told myself I gave it to Gina because I couldn't care less what she thought of me or if she believed me; which was not true. She didn't say a word to me when she first handed it back, she just smiled and nodded her head, which I reckon ended up being better than a whole pile of words. Then she added that a lot of what I'd written was one long paragraph. "Fix it up," she said. "Didn't you ever listen to what Miss said about punctuation?" Then she smiled again and winked at me.

AN ENDING AND A BEGINNING

Over the next six weeks I was allowed to visit Lisatoa, at first only twice a week, then whenever I wanted. Six weeks was how long Lisatoa's mum had grounded him and the only place he could go to was school. Dr Petroni still sent Lisatoa down to Sydney, just to make sure, but he was back in a few days. Where the back of his head had been shaved a row of black stitches had begun to slowly disappear into the growing ginger stubble of his hair.

When I first went to visit Lisatoa at his house it was Iosepha, his dad, who opened the door. He stepped towards me and I thought he was going to give me a hug, but instead he placed his hands on each side of my head, then grabbed the end of my left arm and gave it a shake, all the while nodding his head and grinning widely. "It's not a maybe, it's a definite," were his only words. It made me wonder all over again as to what had happened that night in room 21. I don't think I'll ever be able to work it out, and I'm fine with that. Lisatoa wasn't any help in explaining things either. We were sitting on the verandah, bright morning sun glinting off camphorwood leaves, when I told him about the strange things that night. He listened like it was some interesting story that he'd never heard before, and at the end he just shook his head and said it was all news to him, neither his parents or sisters had said anything of the sort. I told him about our trying to pull him back out of the dark. When I said how we wanted to chain him to us, to everyone in room 21, and to pull him back, he said, "Rope, not chain."

Lisatoa and I both turned twelve at the end of that year. On my birthday mum handed me another of my dad's postcards, along with a small package. The postcard was another photo of a Surfers Paradise beach. I opened the package and inside it was another photo, two young boys standing on a sunlit verandah, wide smiles on sunburnt faces. "My stepsons," he'd written on the back of the photo, "they'd like to meet you." I'd seen photos of them before. I looked closely at the two boys and for the first time it didn't hurt or bother me. Along with the photo there was some ten-dollar notes, "travel money".

"You can visit him if you like," mum said. "You know he loves you." I thought back to that time when Lisatoa and I had gone to Mrs M with the diaries and what she'd said about Alex and his father who'd died. She'd said how you can't bring a dad back, but Alex needs to know he was loved. It was different for me, I could bring a dad back, I could go see him. And if I thought about the dozens of cards he'd sent me, never answering a single one, then maybe he did love me. I also thought about how mum always said how she and my dad separated from each other, not from me. I thought about Lisatoa, lying on that hospital bed and how I didn't want to lose him. I thought about my mum. I might have even thought about Gina for a moment. And I thought how love is a very strange thing, something that can take a zillion forms, some-times a little awkward and messy, sometimes perfect, and how no matter the different shapes and sizes it comes in you should try to never ever lose a single one of them.

"You can visit him if you like," mum said again. "I'm fine with you doing that. Couple of days." And I thought that maybe I would. Yes, yes I would. Just a visit, mind you, a start. I then told mum I was going to answer his postcard, "Be rude not to say thank you for the ten-dollar notes." There was a short silence, then some laughter because we both understood what I meant.

The year that Lisatoa and I turned twelve had been the biggest year I'd ever had. More had happened than I could ever have ex-pected. It was one of the best years of my life. I've had other good years, but that one still stands as one of the best. I wanted to believe how every year would get bigger and better, but even at twelve years old I knew things didn't always work like that. I guess every road has a few bumps and potholes, but the important thing is to keep going because there's a good chance it'll end up being a great journey. Yes, I know that's a metaphor, just felt like sticking one last one in!

Next year it was high school for all of us and Miss' class of 6W would no longer exist. Miss organised an orientation day at the high school, so that we'd know what to expect. But none of it really bothered me, I didn't think and feel too much different to the other kids I'd spoken to. I knew I'd get the usual jokes and problems at the start, but felt I could handle them; they might hurt and upset me, but they couldn't crush me, not anymore. I knew there'd be some surprises, but even they could be good, like when we found out that Miss had a licence to drive the bus that took us to the high school orientation. I didn't know she had any sort of licence. She didn't even grind the gears once.

Lisatoa and I sat at the back of the bus, which was something we wouldn't be able to do next year, that would be for the bigger kids. We were living it up while we could. There was an awful lot of noise going on during that bus ride: everyone chattering, giggling and fidgeting. Kevin was singing "Wheels on the Bus" at the top of his voice, waving the plaster on his newly broken arm about like he was conducting some choir. Someone turned up their transistor trying to drown him out, but Kevin's volume was hard to beat. I didn't know if all that energetic noise was because everyone was excited by the prospect of the high school next year, or just plain glad to be getting close to six weeks summer holiday.

Looking at Kevin's plastered arm made me think once more about Dr Petroni and that night in the hospital. I still had a lot of unanswered questions. I told Lisatoa once more about the stuff with my left hand and asked if he knew anything about it. "Nah," he said, "I reckon that would've been dad. I can't do anything like that." He shrugged his shoulders, then added, "Yet."

Before I could ask any more questions, I saw Gina walking down the aisle of the bus, heading towards the back seat. Miss yelled at her to sit down, which she did, right beside me. And she just sat there, looking straight ahead. I tried to keep my head facing straight ahead too, even while my eyes were straining to see what she was doing. I noticed that she smelt nice, and I thought that was something the big high school kids at the back of the bus would never notice. But what can I say? I noticed.

"Who are you going to the dance with?" Gina asked, still staring ahead. Miss had organised a farewell dance in the school library, a sort of goodbye party. It was going to be on the Friday after the school presentation day where they hand out all the awards for different achievements. The dance wasn't some big formal occasion, it was just for the twenty-six of us in Miss' class. Like I said, it was noisy on the bus, so I didn't say anything. "Who you going to the dance with?" she asked again louder, as if she didn't care who heard.

"I'm not sure," Lisatoa said, "but I'm pretty certain he'll be going with Miss, because they're really good dance partners. They danced at my dad's birthday, so I know this."

Gina ignored Lisatoa. Exactly as she should. "So, for a third time: are you going to the dance with anyone?" I turned my head towards her and saw that she was staring directly at me. Looking back at her I thought, I'm not the boy I was in Sydney, things have changed. I'm the boy who has made a friendship with the boy sitting beside me, better than any friendship anywhere. I'm the boy who helped take a father out of a cave and bring him back to his son. And I'm the boy who will one day visit his father. I'm the boy who rescues gnomes and dogs and rides with Clarry and the Trenchers. I am a singer who brings a friend back home, away from danger, away from hurt. I am the teller of stories, both made up and true. I had become the boy who held Gina's stare and said, "I'm going to the dance with you." Gina said nothing for a moment, smiled and said, "Good, that's settled." She then got up and proceeded back down the aisle, her shiny black hair swaying as she moved. She ignored Miss's yelling. Lisatoa moved around in his seat beside me, cleared his throat and said, "Well, well," and I told him that Gina has very blue eyes.

I'd only been to one presentation day at this school, last year when I was new and in year 5, and it was memorable. The whole school got crammed into the hall, a feat I didn't think possible. The only seats were for parents, and lots of them had to stand. We all had to sit cross-legged on the wooden floor, and I can tell you that can get very uncomfortable, around about the time your legs feel cramped and your bum goes numb. The idea was that everyone would sit quietly and be rivetted while seven teachers spoke about their classes and gave out awards. Really, what kindergarten kid wants to hear about year 6? Or vice versa? Whoever had thought that was a good idea would never be given three hearty British cheers from Miss. Then the weather helped make a bad idea worse. Last year's presentation day was hot and humid, which meant it was like a sauna in the hall. Around the time the leg cramping and bum numbing started, two kindy kids at the front of the hall fainted, just fell sideways like trees felled. The rest of their class began crying. Some kids began talking and it spread like a virus. Lots of giggling and laughter. Some boys started making loud farting sounds, no doubt led by Stephan, and Miss Gunther, the cranky casual teacher, went into the middle of their class and slapped the bare legs of three boys. Other teachers were saying shoosh as loudly as they could, but if anyone heard they didn't do it. Then the three men teachers at the school appeared at the back of the hall, each carrying a cane. They singled out some boys and took them to the side of the hall where they caned each boy twice. It was like a public execution. The hall fell quiet. Apparently, lots of students found the swooshing sound of canes to be quite calming. Whatever teacher was up on the stage at that moment said, "Thank you. That's much appreciated" and I couldn't work out if she appreciated the silence or the caning. It was when the hall was still quiet and the presentations starting up again that a girl in my class, sitting three or four people away on my left, got up on her feet, put a hand across her brow and let out a loud and extended wail before fainting onto the kids beside her. Miss moved towards the fainted student, and with the help of another teacher started to carry her out. As they were carrying her past me, she opened her eyes, looked at me and winked. It was the second wink she had given me and both were very nice. That was the last time we had the whole school in the hall and the first time I really noticed Gina Fontana.

A week before our final assembly Miss spoke to each person getting some sort of award, asking if their parents would be there and if she had the correct spelling of each name that was to go on the awards. I told her that I wanted my first name to be the one my mum had given me. "Bully for you, bully for you," Miss told me.

Our presentation assembly for only years 5 and 6 started with the year 5 teacher talking about how his pupils were going to be the seniors in the school next year and that "the world is your huge oyster" and how it was important to "follow your dreams like determined bloodhounds and shine like sprinkles and dia-monds". Clearly, he had absolutely no writer's streak. When their teacher sat down, I realised once more that we'd been lucky to have Miss as our teacher and I wouldn't have swapped her for any of the others. All these years later, I still think that. Sometimes you have to be saying goodbye to someone or something before you find out how you're going to miss it all.

When Miss got up to speak I knew this would be the last time she'd be talking to us as a class, that a whole phase was just about to end; there would be other shows, but this one was finishing. She spoke about our class and I don't think any of us realised, or believed, how fabulous and wonderful we had been. Miss made us sound like a group of kids that just about anyone would love, which might have been pushing it a bit. She told about times when we could be silly and funny and other times when we could be clever and serious. She named names and told stories, and I started to think that there were people in that class that I might have to add to my list of things I would miss.

Then Miss went all serious and formal when she read out the awards. "Lisatoa Tanuvasa is the recipient of this year's Art Award, an artistic and talented young man. I've even thought I'd like to have some of his drawings hanging in my hallway. Perhaps, I'll just wait to see them in the National Gallery in London. Congratulations Lisatoa." There was absolutely nothing surprising about Lisatoa getting that award; my friend *was* an artist. I looked over at his parents and they looked as proud as could be. Maybe he would get to do some of the illustrations in one of his mum's books. "English," Miss continued, "is the finest language in the world and one of the things it does best is to tell stories. This year's English award goes to Aashray Williams whose narrative rendering of the adventures of Tobias and his mother enthralled the entire class. We all felt as if we were on the ship with them and sharing their "adventurin'". Even though none of the parents knew a thing about my story, there was still a lot of nice clapping. I looked over at my mum and she was using her brightly coloured handkerchief to wipe her eyes.

"Before I announce the dux of the year," Miss continued, "I'd like to make a special award. I think it fitting and, hopefully, a positive sign that my Encouragement Award goes to Alexander MacGregor, who is unfortunately unable to be with us today. He has asked that Aashray collect it for him at the conclusion of presentations." The hall went very quiet. I guess people thought they knew all about Alex. But they didn't. Then, out of the silence, sitting right beside me, Lisatoa began clapping; one person clapping in a crowd can be a lonely sound. Then Gina joined in with him. I followed her, slapping my right hand against the side of my leg. We clapped as loudly as we could. Some others joined in, but it was mainly us three. When we stopped clapping, Miss said, "Finally, we have our dux of Year 6. I've taught quite a few clever students before, but none as likeably mischievous as this year's dux. First in Mathematics, Science, Geography, Craft and History is Gina Fontana." This time lots of people were clapping, and a voice amongst the parents called out, "Brava, Gina, bravissima."

When Miss finished handing out her awards she started to cry, not all loud and weepy, but you could see the shine of welling tears and there was that catch in her voice. Miss was leaving the school, she was going to be a teacher in England, in some village in a place called the Cotswolds. I don't know why, but this made me feel sad, as if because she had been an important part of my life she had no right to pack up and go to the other side of the world. I knew she wasn't going to be my teacher next year, but it felt good to know she would be there, even if I didn't get to see her or be in her class. We might never see our possums again, but I like to know that they're there. Despite finding out that Miss was going away, it had still been a great assembly. And we still had the class party to go.

Gina's house was a big two storey. She didn't live near the river, but on a small block on the outskirts of the town. She said that her house had to be big because her parents "can't stop making babies" and because her grandparents also live there. Walking down her footpath to the front door I could hear music and lots of different voices. How nice it must be, I thought, to live in a house with so much family always around you. Which didn't mean I wasn't happy with my family of two. Just saying that different families might be nice too.

When the front door opened Gina was standing there. She had on a bright red dress, her black hair tied in white ribbons. I wanted to tell her that she looked resplendent, that word I really liked, but without fully knowing why I thought I'd save it for the next time. Standing behind Gina was her dad, and further down the hallway I could see half a dozen craning heads. Gina looked different out of her school uniform and I guess she must have thought the same about me. "Finishes at nine-thirty, right?" her father asked. Gina nodded and her father said, "Good. You will walk her back here, Ray." It wasn't a question.

We walked to the dance in silence. You'd think this would have been awkward and embarrassing, but I felt very comfortable; it just seemed nice to be walking to the school dance with Gina beside me. It was just before eight o'clock, a windless evening with the sky a darkening blue and the heat draining away. Cicadas singing the day out. The smell of frangipani in the front yards of houses. Like I said, it was nice.

The dance was okay. You really can't expect too much to happen with just twenty-six students in a school library for an hour and a half. But I do remember two things that happened. One was talking to Miss; Lisatoa, Gina and I made sure we got to say goodbye to her. She sounded really excited about her trip; she would be going to London, "the capital of the world", then visiting places like Snowdonia, Stonehenge, the Highlands and lots of other places I don't remember. I felt good for her, especially when she said she'd be back in a year and would want to know how high school had been, "Because you two boys have special talents and I want to hear how they have grown. And Gina, you can be a naughty and mischievous thing, but you are so talented and really quite wonderful that I suspect you will always get away with it!" The other thing I remember is that Gina and I had three dances, and I quite liked it and didn't think about any other things, just the dancing. Perhaps, it was part of Gina being really quite wonderful.

It was at the very end of the evening when Kevin sang Auld Lang Syne; he sang the Scottish version, so I didn't understand the meaning of almost any of the words. But somehow I knew ex-

178

actly what the song was about. And I wasn't the only one. The complete silence when Kevin finished was the best applause he could ever have hoped for.

Lisatoa and I walked beside Gina, the three of us slowly heading towards her house. We talked about next year. I'd said it before, but I went over it again about how there'd be lots of changes, how we'd be nobodies in a big alien school, how we'd be stepping into the big wide world. "Seems like we've got such a long, long way to go. Could be exciting." I said.

"When you have to lay a thousand bricks," Gina said, "it all begins with the first one. My dad tells me that. He also says I should stop whinging and get on with it."

"Yeah," Lisatoa said, "we'll be fine. Been through bigger things. Besides, lots have done it before us. Nah, we'll be just fine, Ray. Our gang of two will do okay."

"Correction," Gina said, "it will be a gang of three."

And that sounded just about right to me. All of it.

I have finished cooking my Rajasthani onion and potato curry. I am quite pleased with it, though I don't think I'm developing a chef's streak. However, I think you should try cooking something like it if you have the ingredients and the need.

ABOUT THE AUTHOR

Ian Jamieson has spent his working life being an English teacher, a career he settled on because he liked books and reading, and figured he'd get to do a lot of both. And get paid. It seemed a good plan at the time, and one that has mostly worked out. Previously, Ian has been a paper boy in London, a bricklayer's labourer, a fencer, a greyhound walker, a gardener, and factory worker. Teaching suited him the best.

Ian has an MA and a PhD. He enjoys taking long walks and cycling, but it's reading and writing he enjoys most. *Not Missing a Single Thing* is the first novel Ian has had published. He has written several other novels, but he says they sit in a dark and dusty bottom drawer, exactly where they belong. He is currently working on a new novel, which he hopes will avoid that bottom drawer. Ian lives on a small acreage at the base of the Razorback Range.

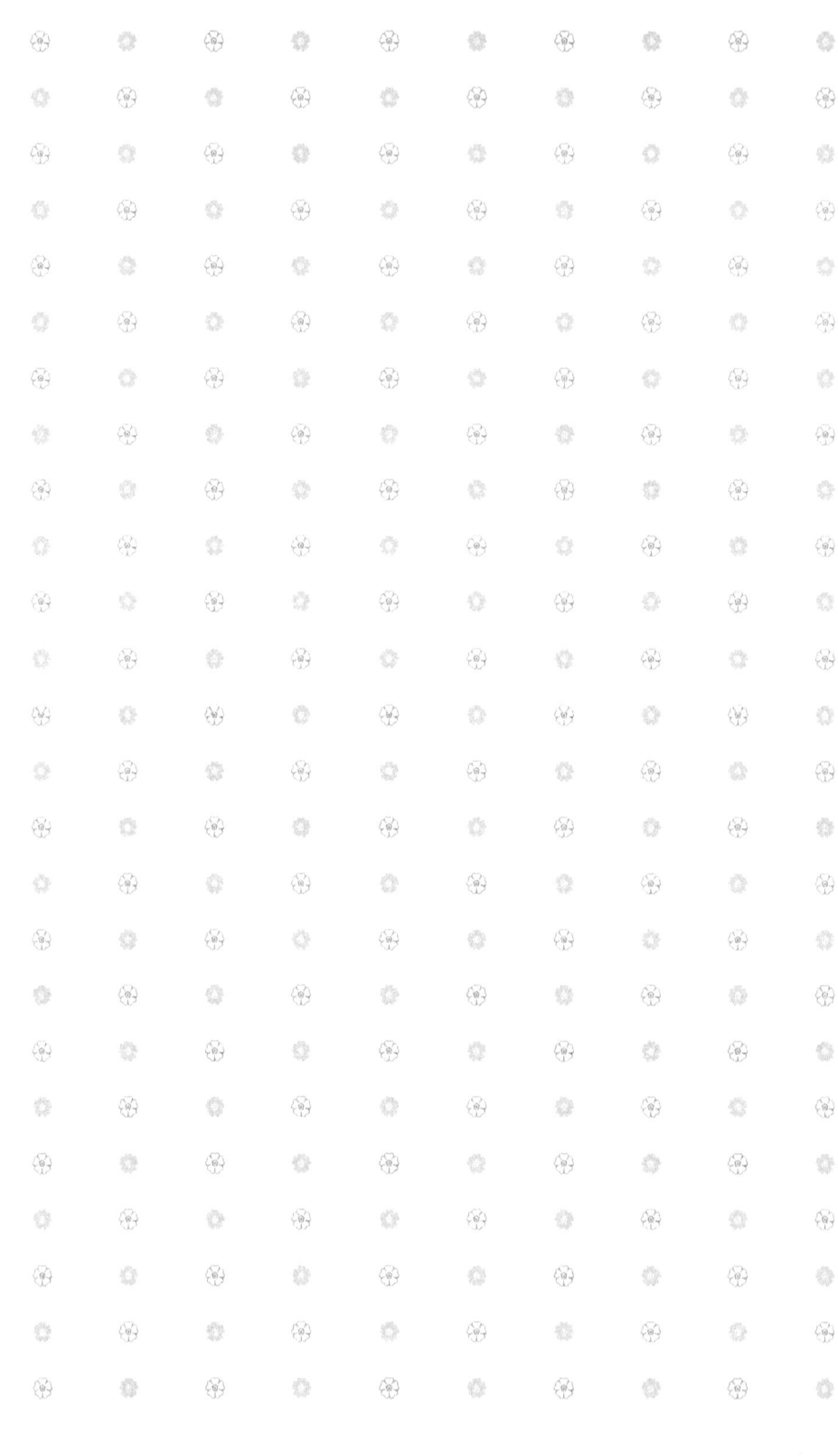